SLAY BELLS RING

An Annabelle Archer Wedding Planner Mystery #17

LAURA DURHAM

Broadmoor Books

CHAPTER ONE

"Are you sure you don't want to join us?" I asked my assistant, Kate, as I knelt under the Christmas tree and gathered the few wrapped presents into a large paper shopping bag.

"And crash your first Christmas as a married woman visiting your parents?" Kate grinned at me from over a large red mug as she sat on my couch with her bare feet tucked under her. "I wouldn't dream of it."

I sighed, thinking of spending the next few days with my parents and new husband, Detective Mike Reese. Even though my parents adored him—especially my mother—I'd hoped to spend our first Christmas as husband and wife at our apartment in Washington, D.C. Life had been a whirlwind since our summer wedding, and because of an ill-timed hurricane, we hadn't even taken a proper honeymoon yet.

I'd thought the few days around Christmas would be the perfect time to curl up around the Christmas tree, drink hot cocoa, and watch the snow fall. Unfortunately, my mother had managed to guilt me into driving down to Charlottesville with the reasoning that she and my father hadn't seen us since our wedding. I'd agreed only because I was afraid that if I didn't, she might show up unannounced with enough Victorian holiday decor to send my cop husband running for the hills.

"Richard is coming," I told Kate, as I stood and bumped one of the fir branches of the tree, making the red and gold glass ornaments shake. "Since his significant other is still on assignment overseas, it's just the three of us driving down. There's room for you in the car."

Kate swiped at the whipped cream on her upper lip. "Your mother and Richard are new BFFs. Me she tolerates."

"That's not true. My mother likes you."

Kate raised an eyebrow and brushed a hand through her blond bob. "She would like me more if I wore skirts that covered my knees and tops that didn't show cleavage."

That was true. My gaze went to Kate's long legs—bare even though it was freezing outside—and I smiled as I thought of the scandalized look that would have crossed my mother's face. My Southern belle mother hadn't adapted to my assistant's fondness for miniskirts and push-up bras. Then again, she also hadn't made her peace with me wearing my auburn hair up in a messy ponytail most of the time and yoga pants around the house. "You know you'd be welcome. What are you doing for Christmas, anyway?"

Kate gave me a mischievous grin. "Don't worry about me, Annabelle. I have plans."

"That's exactly what I'm worried about." I carried the paper bag to the door and set it beside the duffel bags and rolling suitcases that were already packed for our drive. "There aren't any yuletide bar crawls or Santa speed dating events, are there?"

Kate laughed. "I promise I'll behave. Besides, someone has to be on call in case our bride needs anything."

I groaned. "How did we get roped into another New Year's Eve wedding? I swore that we wouldn't take one after the last time."

As the owner of Wedding Belles, one of the city's most

successful wedding planning firms, I'd done my fair share of weddings over the holidays, and every time I swore that each one would be my last. Even though weddings on New Year's Eve were festive and had a built-in theme, planning them meant we couldn't take off fully during the Christmas holidays. One week before the wedding was the time when final numbers were due to the caterer and seating assignments were sent off to the calligrapher. That meant we couldn't put up an away-from-office message and completely relax.

"I'm pretty sure it was the big, fat check," Kate said, waving a hand at the colorfully wrapped boxes remaining under the tree. "Someone has to pay for all those presents."

"You're sure it's okay to do our usual Wedding Belles holiday party after I get back? I'd hoped we could squeeze it in before today, but Reese has been working like crazy in order to get time off on Christmas Eve and Christmas Day."

Kate waved a hand at me. "It's fine. You'll be back the day after Christmas. Everyone thinks it's fun we're having a Boxing Day party, even if they don't know what it is."

"It's a British holiday that started when the aristocracy would take boxes of—"

"Yeah, yeah," Kate said. "I know it's a really old British thing, but let me imagine it's a day celebrating sweaty, muscular guys wearing nothing but shiny shorts and boxing gloves."

I rolled my eyes. Kate's fondness for any type of guys—sweaty or otherwise—was legendary. Despite working as a wedding planner with me, she was a serial dater who rarely went out with the same man for more than a few weeks. But I did have to admit she'd slowed her pace recently.

"Speaking of your hottie cop husband, isn't he supposed to be here soon? I thought he wanted to get out of the city before the snow started."

"We're only supposed to get a dusting," I said, even though

Kate was right. Reese was supposed to have been home an hour ago.

"You know what a dusting of snow does to D.C. People lose their minds."

She was also right about that. D.C. residents did not know how to drive in the snow, and the city practically shut down at the first sign of flakes. "It's fine. My mother isn't expecting us until after dinner."

Kate did not look convinced, but she took another sip of her hot chocolate, closing her eyes as she swallowed. "This can't be Swiss Miss. Did you treat yourself to that Williams-Sonoma hot chocolate?"

I shook my head, heading toward my kitchen. "Nope. It's actually a mix that one of our neighbors dropped off as a holiday present."

"You exchange presents with your neighbors?" Kate twisted around to watch me through the divider between the living room and kitchen. "I didn't know you were friendly with anyone other than Leatrice and Sidney Allen."

"This is the first year any of our neighbors have given out gifts." I picked up the large Mason jar from the counter and twisted off the top that was decorated with a red-and-green-striped bow, pouring a small amount of the dark brown powder into a mug. "Don't you remember that couple I told you about? They started it with the cocoa mix, then Leatrice and Sidney Allen gave out splits of apple cider because Sidney Allen can't stand being one-upped when it comes to Southern customs."

"Is it the preppy couple?" Kate asked.

"Mindy and Kurt." I nodded. "The woman either spends a lot of time on Pinterest or went to some sort of finishing school. My mother would love her."

"Then I'm assuming we hate her?" Kate tapped a finger against her chin. "I think I remember you mentioning them."

"We don't hate her," I said. "I barely know them. They moved in to the second floor about six months ago."

A flash of recognition crossed her face. "Does the guy have tattoos and ride a motorcycle?"

I lifted the still-hot kettle off the stove and poured steaming water into my mug. "Not by a long shot. That's the guy on the third floor. He owns a bar."

Kate's eyes flared with interest. "That explains why we've only run into him when we're coming back late from weddings."

I unwrapped a candy cane and used it to stir my hot chocolate then hooked it over the side of the mug. "I think he sleeps during the day. At least that's what Leatrice says."

"Let me guess. Your resident spy wannabe has him under surveillance?"

My first-floor neighbor, Leatrice, was over eighty, recently married to a quirky entertainment director she met at one of my weddings, and was convinced that half of D.C.—including most of our neighbors in Georgetown—were spies. She preferred listening to her police scanner instead of the radio and owned a rich assortment of spy gear herself, not to mention various costumes so she could follow people undetected.

"Not anymore." I joined Kate in the living room again, taking the overstuffed chair across from her. "After a week of him doing nothing but coming home late and not emerging until the afternoon, she got bored. Luckily, she always has Mr. Kopchek."

Kate sighed. "She isn't still convinced that little old man is a Russian sleeper, is she?"

"He doesn't do himself any favors by being such a grump." I took a sip of my pepperminty hot chocolate, the rich flavor instantly soothing. "He's always complaining that people are playing their music too loudly. He even leaves notes for Mindy and Kurt about Kurt's bike, and they keep that on the first floor with Leatrice's permission."

"I guess it is a pain to haul a bike upstairs," Kate said. "But you know there's someone like that in every building. Don't you

66666666

remember the lady I told you about in my apartment building? The one who uses her cane to poke people in the elevator?"

"At least you have an elevator."

Kate scooted a pile of wedding magazines over and put her mug on the crowded coffee table. "Believe me, I know firsthand what a pain it is that you live in a walk-up, but at least you're on the fourth floor. I'm on the eighth. And your neighbors may be a little nutty, but there aren't many of them."

My apartment building was located in the upscale neighborhood of Georgetown, and like most things in Georgetown, it was only a few stories high and was more charming than modern. Each of the floors of the stone-front building held two apartments, so there were fewer than fifteen residents in total.

"But does your cane lady give out written citations?" I asked.

"Citations?"

I nodded. "Somehow Mr. Kopchek has printed citations. I've gotten them when I've parked too far from the curb or walked up the stairs too loudly."

"I'm surprised I haven't gotten one."

"Me, too," I said. Kate was a horrible driver and even worse at parking. "Although the written citations are new. Keep parking with one tire up on the curb, and you'll get one soon enough."

Kate shivered. "That reminds me of that old mother-of-the-bride who used to write down infractions in her notebook."

I took a big gulp of my warm drink. "Don't remind me of her."

"Because she was killed?" Kate whispered, even though we were the only two people in my apartment.

"That and she was an awful person. Mr. Kopchek isn't like her. He's just a little quirky."

"Then he should fit right in," Kate muttered. "Leatrice and her husband Sidney Allen left quirky in the rearview mirror a long time ago."

"I just don't get why Leatrice is convinced the old man is a spy," I said. "Wouldn't a real spy keep a lower profile? Have you ever heard of a sleeper agent who gives out neighbor citations?"

"No," Kate admitted. "But I'm not up on my spy trivia either. It would be a pretty good double feint for a spy to be a total nuisance."

"In that case, Leatrice is definitely a spy."

Kate snorted a laugh. "If she hears you say that, she'll be thrilled."

My phone buzzed in my jeans pocket, and I pulled it out, staring at the screen for a moment before looking up at Kate. "Richard is searching for parking. Why would Richard be running late? He never runs late."

Kate took out her own phone and swiped her finger across the screen. "This is what happens when we don't have a wedding a few days away, and we aren't checking the weather every hour." She held up her screen, and I could make out the weather app and the image of ice-blue snowflakes. "It started snowing two hours ago."

I jumped up and ran to the window overlooking the street, pulling back the yellow curtains and peering down. Snow was falling heavily, and the cars lining the narrow streets were already covered in white. "I can't believe it."

Kate joined me at the window. "The snow that was supposed to be a dusting is now going to be a blizzard."

"So, we're snowed in?" I squinted at a figure in the snow below us struggling with an armful of bags, my breath catching when I recognized the designer duffel. "And it looks like Richard has brought everything he owns."

"No way are you three making it out of the city now." Kate patted me on the back. "This should be cozy."

I rubbed my temples as I counted the number of bags in Richard's arms. "I think you mean crowded."

CHAPTER TWO

"What do you mean we aren't going?" Richard dropped his bags on the floor and droplets of melted snow flew up. He pushed back the hood of his snow jacket to reveal miraculously unruffled dark hair.

"You did come from outside, right?" Kate asked from her perch on the couch.

Richard shot her a look as he shifted his crossbody bag, and a tiny black-and-brown mop of fur poked out of one end. His Yorkie, Hermès, scanned the room and yipped happily when he saw us. "Of course, I did, but we aren't going to let a little snow stop us, are we?"

"A little snow?" I tousled the dog's head. "You do know it's supposed to be a blizzard now, right?"

Richard set the leather bag with his dog on the couch, and Hermès spilled out, revealing that he was wearing a red plaid holiday sweater. He scampered from one end of the couch to the other and walked over Kate. "No, I do not know. Hermès and I have been on our way over here for the past hour."

"And you didn't hear the weather on the radio?" Kate asked. "Or look out the window?"

Richard narrowed his eyes at her. "I'll have you know that Hermès and I don't listen to the radio in the car. We're using drive time to learn French."

Kate rubbed the little dog's belly as he flopped over next to her. "Why am I not surprised by this?"

"Well, the storm front that was supposed to skirt by D.C. shifted suddenly, and now we're getting all the snow that was going to be heading for Pennsylvania." I took Richard's wet coat after he shrugged it off. "It won't let up for at least twenty-four hours."

"Twenty-four hours?" He gazed around him then at the bags he'd brought. "So that means we're not having Christmas in Charlottesville with your mother?"

"It would take us hours to even get out of the city at this point," I told him, hanging his coat on the rack by the door.

"You're right about that," he muttered. "Washingtonians cannot drive in the snow."

Kate picked up her mug from the coffee table and lifted it into the air. "At least we have lots of delicious hot chocolate."

Richard's eyes widened. "You don't mean we're staying *here*." He glanced around my apartment.

Although it was decorated with a Christmas tree and smelled faintly of pine and peppermint, the apartment also had tables covered with my husband's paperwork and my wedding files. Since we'd been planning to be away and not have guests over the holidays, I hadn't bothered to clean. Not that I cleaned that often, anyway.

"You want to try to drive back across town in this?" Kate asked. "I know I'll never be able to make it up Connecticut Avenue without running out of gas first."

I suspected Kate was not exaggerating since she was notorious for driving on fumes.

"We're spending Christmas *here*?" Richard asked again.

I tried not to be offended at his horrified tone. "At least

tonight. Unless you and Hermès want to trek to the nearest Metro station, which isn't very close to us."

"But," Richard spluttered, "I didn't prepare for this." He waved a hand at me. "You aren't prepared for this. Tomorrow is Christmas Eve, and you probably don't have a thing to eat."

I opened my mouth and closed it again. He was absolutely right. Since we were going to my mother's for Christmas, I hadn't stocked the kitchen. There was no turkey in the freezer, no pies cooling on the counter, and no cranberry sauce bubbling on the stove.

Richard pulled out his own phone, dialing as he paced a small circle and mumbled to himself about what a disaster this was. No surprise that he considered my lack of food the most heinous part of the situation since he was the founder and owner of Richard Gerard Catering, one of Washington's most elite caterers.

"I thought I heard barking." My downstairs neighbor Leatrice walked in through the still-open door, her eyes lighting on Hermès getting a belly rub from Kate. "There's the boy I'm babysitting."

I eyed Leatrice's dress which was printed with green tree branches, lights, and ornaments. "You almost match our tree."

She beamed at me. "It's called Christmas tree camo. I'm supposed to be able to stand next to a Christmas tree and blend in."

Glancing down at her feet, I saw that she wore slippers that looked like brightly wrapped presents with bows. Not her most outrageous footwear by a long shot, and it completed the person-as-Christmas-tree look.

"Christmas tree camouflage." Kate tilted her head. "Is this part of your spy gear?"

Leatrice giggled. "Oh, no. This is just fashion."

Even though Richard was talking on the phone in low,

urgent tones, he glanced up and made a derisive noise in the back of his throat. "If that's fashion, I'm Jason Momoa."

"I wish," Kate said under her breath.

If Leatrice heard Richard's comment, she ignored it. Honestly, I thought her Christmas tree camo was the least shocking thing about her. She'd dyed her hair bubblegum pink for my wedding and had decided to grow it out since then. Although I was used to seeing Leatrice with hair dyed jet-black (or occasionally platinum blond or pink), apparently her natural hair color was a snowy white. So, her Mary Tyler Moore flip was white from her roots to her jawline, then the bottom half was a vivid shade of pink.

"You won't need to babysit Hermès anymore," I told her as she sat down on the couch. "Richard isn't going anywhere."

Her face fell. "But I had so many fun activities planned for us."

"None of us are going anywhere," I said, picking up my mug from the coffee table, sidestepping Richard, and heading to the kitchen. "Not in this weather."

"You and the detective aren't going to your parents' house anymore?"

I hadn't talked to my husband yet, but I suspected he wouldn't want to risk our safety or sanity by attempting to drive out of D.C. in a blizzard.

"It's all settled," Richard announced as he slipped his phone in his pocket. "I talked to your mother. She's disappointed but she understands."

"*You* talked to my mother?" I put my dirty mug on the counter, suddenly wishing I had something to make the hot chocolate Irish.

Richard sniffed and touched a hand to his hair. "Gwen and I talk all the time, Annabelle. She's on speed dial."

I didn't think my mother was on *my* speed dial. "Thanks, I guess."

"You're welcome, darling." Richard walked into the kitchen. "I also put in an emergency call to my kitchens. You know we do a lot of holiday drop-offs, so the chef and his staff are still cooking. They're putting food for us on the next truck."

"You didn't have to do that."

Richard's gaze swept the kitchen. "Oh, I think I did."

"This is so exciting." Leatrice clapped her hands from the other room. "We all get to spend Christmas together."

Richard frowned as he glanced through the opening between the two rooms and saw Leatrice's white-and-pink head bobbling above the back of the couch. "I forgot about Leatrice and Sidney Allen. Of course, they're going to invite themselves. Some people just don't know when they're overstepping." He sighed and took his phone out of his pocket. "I hope you don't mind that I'm having linens sent over since you don't own a decent tablecloth. A holiday toile."

"Toile?" The French-inspired pastoral print seemed an odd choice for the holidays. "Does this have anything to do with your recent French obsession?"

He sniffed. "You know it's easier to plan with a theme."

"Is the theme for our snowbound Christmas everything French?"

He gave a me a weary look. "I prefer Christmas in the Chateau."

"Of course, you do," I mumbled. Reese was going to love this.

He pressed his phone to his ear. "If we're hosting interlopers, I'll need to add more food to our order. And lots more wine."

The door swung open, and my husband stepped inside and flipped back the gray hood of his wool coat. His eyes widened slightly as he took in Leatrice, Kate, and Hermès on the couch. His gaze went to the bags clustered around the door and then to me and Richard in the kitchen. His mouth twitched at the corners. "Anything I should know, babe?"

Before I could answer, Richard bustled out of the kitchen

toward him. "Change of plans, Detective. I've called Annabelle's mother and told her that we're snowed in. But don't worry. I promise we won't starve to death. My kitchens are delivering food to feed all of us for at least two days." He swept an arm wide. "It will be a festive Christmas at the Chateau."

"Chateau?" My husband stared. "Two days?"

I followed Richard out of the kitchen and wrapped my arms around Reese. Even though his coat was still cold from being outside, just wrapping my arms around him made me feel better. "Or until the roads are passable. We can't send them out in this now."

He lowered his head to mine and kissed me softly. "We can't?"

I gave him a playful swat on the arm and laughed. I knew he was fond of my friends, even if they were a little prone to dramatics. "You really want to turn people away from the inn on Christmas?"

He frowned, although his hazel eyes danced. "I do see your point. That's not a good look for us, is it?"

"Think of it this way," I whispered. "At least I'm not doing the cooking."

"That is a plus."

I swatted him again. "You were supposed to disagree with me."

He wrapped his arms around me. "You know I would never lie to you, babe."

Richard made an impatient noise. "I hope you two aren't going to be like this the entire time."

"Give them a break." Kate grinned at us. "They're still newlyweds."

"Speaking of lovebirds," Leatrice bounded up from the couch as her own husband appeared at the door.

Sidney Allen wasn't much taller than Leatrice, who barely topped five feet. But whereas Leatrice was skin and bones, her husband was all curves. He almost always wore dark suits with his pants hitched up so high they flirted with his armpits, and when he was coordinating entertainment for an event, he wore a wireless headset so he could shriek orders into it. Luckily, he did not have a headset on at the moment.

Leaning one plump hand against the doorframe, he drew in a long breath as his gaze locked onto my husband, his face flushed. "I'm glad you're here, Mike. I need to report a crime."

Richard put a hand to his heart. "Will the catastrophes ever stop?"

CHAPTER THREE

My husband's face became serious as he studied Sidney Allen's disheveled appearance. "What kind of crime?"

Sidney Allen puffed out his chest, which made it rival the girth of his stomach. "I've been threatened, and the good name of my wife has been tarnished."

Reese's shoulders relaxed a bit. "What kind of threat? Was there a weapon involved?"

"Or just a disgruntled performer?" Richard said so only I could hear him.

He had a point. Sidney Allen was known for being a diva on-site and for bossing around his performers, which he gave code names appropriate to the event. I wouldn't have been shocked if Dickens Caroler #5 had lost their temper and made idle threats.

Sidney Allen smoothed his thinning hair over his forehead and cleared his throat. "No weapon, but he did shake his finger at me."

"My poor Honeybun." Leatrice took him by the arm and pulled him inside, patting his hand as she led him to the couch.

Reese took off his coat and hung it up, then tugged off his boots and left them by the door, the melting snow creating tiny puddles. "I'm not sure if you need a Metropolitan Police Department detective for this kind of thing. It sounds more like a domestic disturbance."

Sidney Allen looked scandalized as he sank onto the couch, and both Kate and Hermès got up. "That makes it sound sordid."

"Why don't you tell the detective what happened?" Leatrice prodded, gazing upon her husband like he'd hung the moon.

"I'll grab you a beer," I said, seeing how torn Reese looked between sitting in the living room and turning around and running back out the door. I suspected he might have made a run for it if it hadn't been snowing so hard.

He gave me a quick squeeze and reluctantly made his way to the chair across from Leatrice and Sidney Allen. "I'm happy to listen, but I'm technically off duty."

I walked to the kitchen as Sidney Allen launched into his tale, which I could tell was going to be long-winded. Kate followed me, hopping up onto the counter and letting her legs swing below her as I opened the refrigerator door.

"At least it isn't a murder," she said. "I don't know if I could handle a blizzard and a murder."

"You've handled a wedding and a murder before. And a vacation and a murder." I grabbed one of my husband's favorite microbrews from the door of the fridge, making note of the sadly stocked shelves. I really should be grateful my best friend was a caterer and that he'd gotten stuck with us. Otherwise, we would have been eating leftover Thai food, yogurt, and some tired grapes for the holidays.

"True." Kate bobbled her head. "But it would be nice if we could avoid dead bodies for a while."

"It's been months since we found a dead body."

"I wouldn't go bragging about that. A lot of people never stumble across corpses."

"Now you sound like my husband. You know better than anyone that we never go looking for trouble."

"Maybe you're right." Kate shrugged then smiled at me. "It still sounds funny to hear you refer to Reese as your husband."

It had taken a while for me to get used to the tall, dark, and handsome detective being my boyfriend and then my fiancé, but calling him my husband had definitely taken the most getting used to. "It *has* been five months."

"I know." She fluttered a hand at me. "It just makes you seem so grown up."

"Speaking of maturing," I said, seeing the opening I'd been looking for, "you haven't mentioned a hot date in a while. Since before my wedding, actually. What gives? Are you really just seeing the same mystery man?"

Spots of pink appeared on her cheeks. "I don't want to jinx it."

"And telling me about him will jinx it?"

She twitched one shoulder up. "I don't know. You know the last time I was serious about someone, it didn't work out."

Kate had told me that she'd once been engaged, and her fiancé had cheated on her. It had soured her on serious relationships and been the reason she'd had the social life of a butterfly ever since.

"Not all guys are cheaters and liars," I said, my gaze going to my husband in the living room as he listened to Sidney Allen.

"I know." She craned her neck to follow my line of sight. "You got a good one."

"This secret guy of yours must be a good one if he's kept you monogamous for so long."

She laughed. "He's definitely different from my usual type." She slid off the counter. "Who knows? Maybe I'll introduce him soon."

With that, she left the kitchen. I followed behind her, my interest piqued.

"And then Mr. Kopchek accused my Honeybun of stalking

him," Sidney Allen said as I crossed the living room and handed my husband a beer.

He smiled up at me then pulled me down into his lap before returning his attention to Sidney Allen. "Who's Mr. Kopchek?"

"The man who lives in 2B," Leatrice said. "The one who might be a Russian mole."

Reese took a long swig of his beer. "Were you stalking him, Leatrice?"

The pink-and-white-haired octogenarian shifted in her seat. "I don't stalk people. I only surveil them."

Sidney Allen swung his head to her. "You were following him?"

Her already rouged cheeks became even redder. "Only at a distance. I'm surprised he made me."

Richard glanced over from where he stood looking out the window and tapping his toe on the floor. "Why? Is he blind?"

Leatrice squared her shoulders. "I'll have you know I wore a trench coat and a fedora."

"Does the fedora cover all the hair?" Richard asked, looking pointedly at her pink tips.

My husband let out a quiet sigh. "So, our neighbor noticed you following him and brought this to your husband's attention?"

Sidney Allen stared at Leatrice. "I swore up and down to the man that you had no reason to do such a thing." He dropped his voice. "I thought you'd stopped."

Kate exchanged a glance with me from where she'd perched on the arm of the couch opposite Leatrice and her husband. We knew that Leatrice regularly spied on people in our building. She definitely did it less since she'd been married, but she clearly hadn't stopped.

"But I did have a reason," Leatrice insisted. "That man spends a lot of time at the park, which as anyone knows, is a prime spot for making drops or meeting contacts."

Sidney Allen put a hand over his eyes, shaking his head slowly. "I owe Mr. Kopchek an apology. I accused him of making it all up." His voice became almost a whisper. "I called him a liar and threatened to kill him if he ever insulted my wife again."

"You threatened to kill a man?" I couldn't hide the surprise in my voice. Sidney Allen had always been a bit of a diva to work with, but I'd never known him to be violent. Or even threaten violence. For one thing, I didn't think he'd be able to carry out a threat, and there were few people who would be genuinely scared by a threat from the small, pudgy man.

Sidney Allen dropped his hand. "I was upset because the snow canceled a big holiday party at the Willard hotel. I had twenty sugarplum fairies all set to flit around and pass out cocktails, but the blizzard ruined all of that. Now I have twenty angry ladies in leotards and wings stuck at the hotel. Mr. Kopchek caught me as I was coming in and getting off the phone with the sugarplum queen. I'm afraid I wasn't in the best mindset to be a good neighbor." He cut his eyes to Leatrice. "Plus, I thought he was making it all up."

"I'm so sorry, Honeybun," Leatrice said, her voice cracking.

He patted her hand. "This isn't your fault, although I would prefer it if you didn't follow our neighbors. We do have to live here."

"Don't sit where you eat," Kate added, making everyone look confused for a moment.

"I think you mean sh—" Richard started to say before I shot him a look.

Reese drained the rest of his beer. "Trust me; I know that the holidays make everyone a little crazy. We always get a big uptick in crime right around now."

Sidney Allen stood. "Still, my holiday stress is no excuse. My behavior was reprehensible." He hiked his pants up even higher. "I need to go apologize."

Leatrice popped up. "I'll go with you."

He shook his head. "No. This is something I need to do by myself—man-to-man."

Leatrice's face fell. "Are you sure?"

He pressed his lips together and gave a single nod.

"Do you want me to go with you?" my husband asked. "In case things get ugly?"

"You're too kind," Sidney Allen said, his Southern drawl thickening. "But this is something a gentleman must do alone."

He strode out of the door with only the hint of a waddle.

Leatrice sighed and flopped back onto the couch. "Isn't he the most gallant man you've ever met?"

"Mon dieu," Richard muttered.

Reese pulled me closer to him. "How long is this blizzard supposed to last again, and how much beer do I have?"

CHAPTER FOUR

"Forget I said anything about there not being enough booze."
My husband staggered into the building as I held the front door
open, the cold air whipping around us both and sending wet
snow flying around the small foyer. He carried three cardboard
boxes, and his eyes barely poked above the top one.

"Is that all wine?" I gaped at the boxes that were making his
knuckles turn white.

"It could be cinder blocks," he said, his breath visible in
the air.

"Do you want me to take one?"

He shook his head, then motioned behind him. "I've got this.
There's more in the truck."

As Reese started up the stairs, I peered through the glass
panes of the door into the swirling snowstorm beyond. One of
Richard's catering trucks was double-parked in front of the
building, its flashers blinking and glowing red through the
white haze. There was a well-worn path through the snow to
the truck, and I could make out two figures at the back—one of
them was Richard and one was the driver.

"'Scuse me." The voice behind me made me step back. The

tall skinny man wore a red knit cap and carried a matching deflated pizza carrier by his side. I recognized him as one of our building's regular pizza delivery guys.

"You're delivering pizzas?" I asked, cutting a glance outside. "In this?"

He shrugged. "People gotta eat. Besides, I get better tips in bad weather."

"Then you should make a killing tonight."

He made a face. "Not from that old guy." He jerked his head up toward the staircase. "He never does more than tell me to keep the change."

I assumed he was talking about Mr. Kopchek since no one else in the building over the first floor could be considered old. The delivery guy muttered something about cheapskates before pushing out into the cold. The door had almost closed when I saw a couple running for it and held it open.

"Thanks!" The woman I recognized as one half of "Mindy and Kurt" from the second floor bustled inside with a duffel bag bouncing on one hip.

Kurt came in after her, dragging a suitcase behind him and stomping his feet to loosen the snow on his boots. "So much for the Caribbean for Christmas."

"You were supposed to go to the Caribbean?" Now I didn't feel so bad about missing our trip to Charlottesville.

Mindy nodded. "The airports have shut down. Not that we even made it that far."

"It's a mess out there." Kurt pushed back the hood of his coat to reveal pale hair that was already starting to thin. "I hope you weren't planning on going anywhere."

I shrugged my shoulders. "Not anymore, unfortunately."

"Same." Mindy ran a hand through her chestnut brown hair and frowned as she glanced up at the staircase. "Now we're stuck here."

"At least we have your hot cocoa to keep us warm," I said. I'd already written a thank you note and slipped it under their door, but I felt like I needed to thank them in person. "It's delicious, by the way."

Mindy gave me a distracted smile. "It's definitely cocoa weather." She motioned to Kurt with her head as she started up the stairs. "We'd better unpack these bags and crank up the heat again."

"Good luck," I called after them, knowing how temperamental the heating units in our older building could be and how they resisted a cold start.

"Look alive, Annabelle!" Richard yelled from the other side of the front door.

I pushed it open so he could enter. Richard groused a bit about my lack of focus, mumbled what was most certainly a curse word in French, and unloaded a canvas bag into my arms, leafy produce poking out from the top.

"Is that everything?" I asked, as Richard shook his feet over the vinyl floor.

"Darryl has the rest," he said, nodding toward the truck and the figure unloading at the back that I assumed was Darryl.

I hesitated about letting the door go since Darryl would need to be able to get into the building, but my fingers were also starting to freeze from standing half in and half out of the building. A gloved hand grabbed the door from the outside and pulled in open, making me stagger back a bit.

"Sorry." The man I recognized as the bar owner from the third floor came inside followed by a heavily bundled man carrying two armloads of bags—Darryl, I assumed.

Richard was already halfway up the first flight of stairs and barely glanced back as he called out directions. "It's on the top floor. Of course."

The bundled man with bags followed Richard. The bar owner stopped in the foyer with a black motorcycle helmet under one arm, pulled his black cap off, and shook it out, sending icy pellets scattering to the floor. He had brown hair and a face full of scruff with the edge of a dark tattoo curling out from underneath his collar. He was definitely what Kate would consider hot, but in a slightly bad-boy kind of way.

"You look like you're ready to ride this thing out," he said, giving me a lopsided grin.

"I guess," I said, readjusting the canvas bag Richard had given me. "We don't really have much choice."

"I hear that." He tugged off his gloves, waving one at the door. "I had to close the bar before it gets even worse. I didn't want to have a bunch of drunk guys who couldn't get home."

"That makes sense."

The door opened again, and a burly man holding a pair of stacked cardboard boxes stepped inside. "Where does Mr. Gerard want these?"

I blinked at him. Wait, if this was Darryl, who had walked upstairs with Richard?

The bar owner tucked his motorcycle helmet under the stairs and took the boxes from him. "I'll take them. I'm going up anyway."

Darryl grinned, clapping his hands together to warm them up. "Thanks, man. I want to get this truck back to the ware-house while I still can."

"Drive safe," I called after the man's retreating back as he disappeared into the snow.

When I turned, the bar owner had already started up the stairs.

"You don't have to do this," I said.

He twisted his head to look at me, smiling again. "What are neighbors for?"

I smiled back as I followed, thinking that Kate would defi-nitely have been better at this than I was. If she was in my place, she would have been gushing over the guy and probably have set a date with him before she'd reached the top floor. At least, the old Kate would have.

"Thanks," I said. "I'm on the top floor."

"I know," he said. "You're the wedding planner, right?"

How did he know that?

Before I could ask him, he said, "The lady on the first floor talks a lot."

Leatrice. For a spy wannabe, she was extremely chatty.

"I'm Alton," he added as he reached the first landing. "I run the Salty Dog down near the water."

I already knew that—from Leatrice, no less—but I didn't tell him. "Annabelle."

"Nice to officially meet you, Annabelle." He'd stopped in front of one of the doors on the second floor to wait for me, then when I caught up, he let me lead the way. "Isn't it crazy that you can live in the same building as someone and never know them? We must have walked past each other a hundred times."

"D.C.," I said. "Everyone's too busy."

"You got that right. Not that I can complain." He adjusted his grip on the boxes as he fell in step behind me. "People being too busy and too stressed-out keeps my business afloat."

"Mine too."

He barked out a laugh. "I'll bet. Hey, didn't you just get married yourself? To a cop?"

"That's right." I was relieved that he knew I was married. Not that he'd been flirting with me exactly, but I was pretty bad at telling if a guy was being friendly or if it was something more. "He's a detective."

"Lucky us. Not every building gets to have its own built-in security."

I wanted to tell him that with Leatrice we had way more security than we needed, but that required a deeper explanation than I was willing to get into. I was just glad Leatrice wasn't bounding up the stairs with us. After a respectable amount of time, she'd gone after Sidney Allen, and I suspected they were still talking things through in their apartment. I knew the two would reappear at some point. For now, I was enjoying the break.

"So, are you here for the holidays?" I asked as we passed the door to his third-floor apartment. "I mean, I guess you are now whether you wanted to be or not."

He laughed again. "I was always here. The holidays are peak times for my bar. Not now, though. This storm looks like it's going to be a big one."

"I don't know how it snuck up on me. I'm usually on top of the weather."

"In your line of work, I'll bet. I'm guessing you don't have any weddings coming up?" He hesitated. "Or is all this stuff for a wedding?"

"No. Believe it or not, these are just supplies that my caterer friend needs to cook for the next couple of days. We were all supposed to be leaving town, but now we're not. Luckily, my next wedding isn't until New Year's Eve." My stomach tightened. "I hope all this snow has melted by then."

"Don't worry. It's Washington. When does snow ever stick around?"

He had a point. We didn't get lots of snow, and what we did usually melted quickly. Of course, it had been almost a decade since the city had seen a blizzard like this. At least, according to Richard, who had lived here longer than I had. According to my best friend, it had taken almost two weeks for everything to melt the last time there was a blizzard.

I shook my head, as if banishing those thoughts. "I'm sure you're right." We reached the fourth floor and the door to my apartment, which was slightly ajar. "Since you're stuck here over the holidays, too, you're welcome to join us." I nodded to the boxes in his arms. "I'm pretty sure we have enough."

He shook his head. "That's nice of you, but you barely know

me. I don't want to butt in on your Christmas plans."

I nudged open the door with my foot. The theme song to "A Charlie Brown Christmas" was playing from someone's phone while Hermès ran in circles around the couch and Richard unloaded bags in the kitchen. My husband was unpacking bottles of wine onto the dining table while Kate was already uncorking one. A tall bundled-up figure stood next to the door unwinding a long scarf.

"Why does this bag have hair spray in it?" Richard called out as he held an industrial-sized can over his head. "I did not order hair spray."

"That's mine," the bundled man said, removing the scarf completely to reveal himself to be Fern. "You don't expect me to ride out a blizzard with bad hair, do you, sweetie?"

"Sacre bleu," Richard muttered, sounding just as horrified in French as he did in English. "What are you doing here?"

"I had to close my salon." Fern hooked his scarf on the coat rack and patted his pristine dark ponytail. "And I knew I'd never get across town to my own apartment, so I came here."

Kate ran up and threw her arms around him. "Did you bring any other supplies?"

He tapped on his chin and gave her a wicked smile. "I might have emptied the salon's fridge of all the Veuve Clicquot."

Richard held up a champagne bottle with the signature yellow label. "There must be half a case in here."

Kate rubbed her hands together. "Now we're ready for the snow."

I turned to Alton. "See? You don't have to worry about intruding on my quiet Christmas because I won't be having one."

His eyes were wide. "I guess not."

Fern spun around and his gaze landed on Alton. He squeezed Kate's hand as he eyed the handsome bar owner. "Looks like Santa brought us an early present."

CHAPTER FIVE

"I can't believe you invited a complete stranger." Richard's voice was nearly a hiss as he peeked over the space between my kitchen and living room to where Alton sat on the couch rubbing Hermès's belly.

I stood next to my best friend, unpacking bags and trying to find space for the abundance of food in my galley kitchen. The enormous turkey took up so much room in the refrigerator that we'd had to adjust the shelves. For once, it paid off not to have a fully stocked kitchen.

A small saucepan filled with mulling spices was already bubbling on the stove top, sending spicy steam into the air. Richard had explained that this way it would at least smell like Christmas until he was able to cook something.

"It's Christmas," I said. "Besides, he's not a total stranger. He's a neighbor who was going to be alone."

"A neighbor you'd never spoken to before." Richard narrowed his eyes at the back of the man's head. "Although he seems to be making fast friends with my dog."

Even though Richard had always proclaimed his disdain for children and animals, he'd taken to his significant other's Yorkie with surprising enthusiasm, renaming him something more chic than his original name, and dressing him in designer doggie outfits to match his own clothes. Hermès, for his part, had taken to the makeover with great gusto, becoming every bit as fussy as Richard.

"I'm more surprised Kate isn't all over him," I said, watching my assistant chat with Fern across from the couch. "I really think she's changed."

Richard made a noise that told me he wasn't so convinced. "She might just be worn out. She has been dating at a competitive level for years. You can't keep that up without burning out."

I frowned at him. "I'm serious. I think this mystery guy of hers has changed her." I grabbed his arm. "Do you think she might marry him?"

Richard pressed his lips together briefly. "If she gets married before I do…"

"Wait, are you and P.J. serious?" I hadn't spent much time with Richard's significant other since the man traveled frequently for his State Department job, but I did know this was the longest relationship I'd been aware of my best friend having.

Richard turned his attention back to a bag of chestnuts. "Is there any chance you have a colander, darling?"

I scanned the closed cabinets, deciding not to press the question with Richard. For now. "There's always a chance."

He sighed. "I should get hardship pay for this."

Bending over, he dug around in one of the lower cabinets until he produced a metal colander.

"It smells great." My husband poked his head around the doorframe of the kitchen. "What are you cooking?"

"Cinnamon sticks," Richard said.

Reese raised an eyebrow. "Yum?"

Richard sighed. "It's to give a festive scent to the air." He put his hands on his hips and appraised all the ingredients on the counter. "I guess I should make a stew for tonight since

Annabelle's turned your apartment into a soup kitchen. If only I had the ingredients to make a bouillabaisse, it would fit with our theme."

My husband grinned, dropping his voice. "I take it this is about Alton?"

"You know Richard doesn't adapt well to new things. He barely adjusted to you."

Richard gave me a scandalized look. "Bite your tongue. I was always fond of the detective."

Now it was my turn to give him a shocked look. "What? You practically pouted for months when we started dating."

Richard twitched his shoulders. "I don't remember that."

To his credit, Richard had come around to the detective—and then some. Once he'd realized that Reese wasn't going anywhere and he'd have to learn to share me, he'd decided to co-opt him for himself. To his credit, my husband had taken to having a brand-new self-appointed best buddy with complete grace.

"My point is that new things aren't always bad," I said. "This Alton guy helped us carry up all the boxes, and he seems perfectly nice."

Richard cast another quick glance at the brown-haired man. "He's a bar owner. And he has tattoos."

"What's wrong with tattoos?" I crossed my hands over my chest. "They're pretty mainstream now. Everyone has them."

"Mmhmm." Richard dumped the bag of chestnuts into the colander and set it in the sink. He plucked a wooden spoon from a drawer and waved it at me. "Don't think I've forgotten your little dalliance with that tattooed fellow, Annabelle."

My cheeks warmed, and I narrowed my eyes at him. "It wasn't a dalliance. I went out with that guy a few times."

"I'm assuming this was before me?" my husband asked, the amusement clear in his voice.

"Don't worry, Detective," Richard said with a wave of his spoon. "There was only minimal overlap."

"Minimal?" My husband's eyebrows shot up. "Overlap?"

I stepped closer to Richard and dropped my voice to a deadly whisper. "How do you say 'I'm going to kill you' in French?"

Richard's gaze went from me to my husband and his face reddened. "I didn't mean that, Annabelle, I mean, you know she would never actually...When I said overlap, I didn't mean she was dating you both at once. She could barely date one person at a time, much less two." He looked back at me. "You weren't, were you, darling?"

"No," I said, tapping one foot on the floor. "I was not." I swiveled my face to my husband. "*You* hadn't asked me out yet."

"You did take your sweet time, Detective." Richard put a hand to his forehead. "But it's all such a blur. It was so long ago. I'm feeling hot. Is it hot in here?"

I gestured to the steam billowing up from the stove. "You're standing over the mulling spices."

"Oh." He stepped back and fanned himself with the hand not holding the spoon. "I was wondering why my sudden dizzy spell was accompanied by the scent of cloves."

My husband closed the distance between us, wrapping his arms around me from behind. He leaned down and kissed my neck. "Well, I'm glad I finally asked you out. Apparently, I had competition."

"Not really," Richard said. "I never would have let Annabelle carry on with someone who wore leather pants and..." His words drifted off when he caught sight of my face. He took his fingers and pretended to lock up his lips. "Never mind. Don't mind me. I'm going to busy myself with our dinner for tonight."

"Good idea," I said as Reese walked me back toward the doorway. "Don't forget Leatrice and Sidney Allen will probably come back up and join us."

Richard let out a tortured sigh. "I don't know where we're all going to sit."

As my husband and I made our way back out to the living room, I realized that Richard had a point. Our dining table wouldn't seat everyone, especially now that I'd invited our neighbor. Then, again, I didn't mind people sitting around with bowls on their laps. It was how Reese and I ate most of our meals, though I would never admit as much to Richard, who believed eating takeout on the couch should be classified as a misdemeanor at the very least.

"Try this, Annabelle." Kate thrust a glass in my hand.

I eyed the red contents. "What is it?"

She jerked a thumb behind her to where Fern stood at the dining table with an impressive array of liquor bottles in front of him. "We're coming up with a signature cocktail."

"For...?"

She threw her arms wide. "For the blizzard, of course. We haven't settled on a name yet, but we think this is an event that deserves a custom cocktail."

Since almost all of our weddings had a signature cocktail—and couples christened them everything from their dog's name to an odd mash-up of their own first names—it wasn't crazy for Kate to make a custom drink for the blizzard.

"I suggested the Blizzitini," Fern called. "But Kate wants the Snow Gin Fizz."

I swirled the contents of the glass. "Should I ask what's in it?"

"Not before you try it," Kate said. "But don't worry; I kept it simple and clean."

I knew that was code for a ton of alcohol and a splash of mixer. "You should probably let the expert taste it first."

"Fern already tried it," Kate said, tilting her head at me.

"Not Fern, our resident bar owner." I nodded to Alton on the couch, who was still playing with a delighted Hermès.

He looked up. "Did someone say bar?"

Fern clapped his hands together. "Why didn't I think of that? We have an in-house mixologist."

"Why not?" Kate didn't look so convinced. "Fern and I are trying to come up with a custom cocktail. Something to embody the blizzard."

"It's a wedding thing," I said, when I saw the confused look on his face.

"I'm actually not a mixologist, and the Salty Dog serves a lot of beer and whiskey, but I'm always happy to taste something."

I gladly handed him the glass, curious that Kate was watching him with a look she usually saved for bossy bridesmaids. Not only was she *not* flirting, she seemed to be going out of her way to appear uninterested in the good-looking guy.

Before he could take a swig, the door flew open and Leatrice ran in, her hands pressed to her cheeks. "Come on! You have to hurry!"

My husband stiffened behind me. "What's wrong?"

Leatrice heaved in a shaky breath, a small sob escaping from her throat. "I think he's dead!"

CHAPTER SIX

"She's finally killed him," Richard said from the kitchen, his jaw hanging open.

It was no secret that Richard wasn't fond of Sidney Allen. I always suspected that it was the diva principle—you couldn't have two overly dramatic bosses in the same place for too long. And both Sidney Allen and Richard both liked to be in charge. Hence, they weren't crazy about each other.

"What?" Leatrice shook her head, then beckoned us with one arm. "I didn't kill anyone, but you need to hurry."

My husband hurried after her as she disappeared from the doorway, and I followed right behind him. I paused and looked back at Kate. "Maybe you should keep everyone else entertained here." When she opened her mouth to protest, I darted my gaze to Richard then Fern. "If he really is dead, I'm guessing Reese won't want added drama at the scene."

She nodded. "You got it."

Leatrice and Reese were already a flight ahead of me, and I had to run down the stairs to catch up. When I reached the second floor, I almost smacked into my husband's broad back.

"Why did we stop?" I asked.

He was staring through the open door to apartment 2B. Small puddles of water pooled around the door where snow had obviously melted. "This is where Leatrice went."

"Why would Sidney Allen be in here? They live on the first floor."

My husband's face was grave. "I don't think Leatrice is talking about Sidney Allen."

He walked through the open door. I stood in the hallway for an extra beat before following him. I'd never been inside another apartment in my building, aside from the one Leatrice lived in with her Honeybun, but I did know that because it was an older building, each floor plan was different.

Instead of opening into one large living room like mine did, this apartment featured a short hallway that passed a galley kitchen off to one side and then spilled out into a large living-dining combination. An open pizza box lay on the counter between the kitchen and living room, the scent of pepperoni filling the room. The warm glow of a shaded floor lamp illuminated part of the large room, but the heavy, closed drapes made it feel dark. The deep autumnal colors of the furniture didn't help either.

It wasn't the burgundy-and-mustard-yellow plaid couch that drew my attention, however. It was Mr. Kopchek slumped across it that made me stop short and put a hand on the wall to steady myself. A TV tray sat to one side of the couch with a half-eaten slice of pizza and a mug with some sort of corporate insignia on it.

Leatrice stood next to the man, wringing her hands. "I checked under his nose first, and when I didn't feel any breath, I tried for a pulse."

Reese moved deliberately to the man, touching a single finger to the side of his neck and holding it for a few seconds. I didn't need him to shake his head to know that the man was dead. Although his skin wasn't pale or tinged blue like most dead bodies I'd seen, no one slept with their neck at a painfully awkward angle like that.

"You okay, babe?"

I realized that my husband was talking to me. I tore my gaze from the dead body and nodded mutely. Even though I'd seen more than my fair share of dead bodies, the sight never failed to startle me and make me feel a bit queasy. And the rich scent of pizza wasn't helping me fight the urge to puke.

"Did you touch anything?" my husband asked Leatrice when he pulled his hand back.

"Touch? What?" She hadn't wrenched her eyes away from the old man. "I don't think so. I mean, maybe. I don't remember."

Reese let out a breath, his gaze scanning the room. "Why were you in his apartment anyway?"

She glanced up at him, blinking rapidly. "I was coming back up to your place, actually. My Sugar Muffin and I had a long chat. He didn't feel like being around people yet, but I thought I'd check in and see what you kids were up to." She drew a shaky breath. "Mr. Kopchek's door was open, so I knocked."

"The door was standing open?" Reese asked.

Leatrice glanced down. "It might not have been standing open, but it wasn't closed all the way, which I thought was strange."

I saw my husband frown slightly. "So, you knocked. Then what?"

"Then I called his name a few times and told him his door was open." She chanced a look at him again, and her cheeks lost another shade of color. "When I finally walked inside, I saw him just like this. I thought maybe he was sleeping, but then I got closer."

Reese put his hands on his hips. "I don't see any obvious signs of foul play, but you did say his door was open, right?"

Leatrice nodded. "I thought maybe my Honeybun hadn't closed it well when he'd left."

Reese snapped his head to her. "Sidney Allen was here before you?"

Leatrice nodded. "He was coming down to apologize, remember?"

"And did he?" my husband asked.

"He said he did." Leatrice worked her hands together, her painted-on eyebrows pressed together in obvious distress. "You aren't suggesting that my Cupcake had anything to do with this, are you?"

"Isn't this a heart attack or something?" I asked, finally letting myself look at the body again. "It looks like he keeled over."

"Maybe." Reese walked around the room without touching anything. "Even if that's the case, Sidney Allen might have been the last person to see Mr. Kopchek alive."

"This is awful," Leatrice murmured to herself. "First my Honeybun gets in a fight because he's defending my honor, and now the man he argued with is dead."

"What are you going to do?" I asked Reese.

"I have to call it in, but I don't know when an ME will be able to get to us." He rubbed a hand across his forehead. "For now, we need to keep the scene secured until I'm sure it was a natural death. I also need to talk to Sidney Allen."

Leatrice bobbed her head up and down. "We can lock the door. I saw a key hanging by the kitchen."

"Don't touch anything," Reese warned as Leatrice hurried toward the door.

I followed quietly as my husband pulled a pen out of his blazer pocket and used it to hook the key off the wall. We all stepped outside into the hall and let the door close behind us.

"I should go tell my Sugar Pie." Leatrice peered over the stair railing toward the first floor.

"Not yet," Reese told her. "Let's go back upstairs, so I can call this in. Then we'll go talk to Sidney Allen together."

Leatrice didn't look thrilled with this, but she didn't argue. When we reached our apartment, Reese held the door open for us. I was pleased to breathe in the comforting scent of mulling spices. Anything beat the smell of pepperoni and death.

"Well?" Kate jumped up from an overstuffed chair when we walked in. "Is he okay?"

My husband slid the key onto a shelf on the bookcase by the door. "Not exactly."

Kate looked stricken as she stared at Leatrice. "You're not saying that he's …?"

Leatrice nodded. "Dead."

Fern sucked in a breath then rushed over to Leatrice and threw his arms around her. "This is too cruel."

"Sidney Allen isn't dead," I said, watching Leatrice struggle in Fern's smothering hug. "Mr. Kopchek is."

Alton tilted his head at me, taking a momentary break from rubbing a nearly catatonic Hermès's belly. "Mr. Kopchek?"

"Not Sidney Allen?" Fern released Leatrice, and she stumbled toward the couch, patting her disheveled hair.

"The guy we were talking about earlier?" Kate dropped her voice as she sidled closer to me. "The old man Leatrice was stalking?"

Richard came out of the kitchen wearing a Santa apron. "Wait, who's dead?"

"Mr. Kopchek," we all said at once, and Richard jumped.

"He's dead?" Sidney Allen stood in the doorway, his face ashen. "That's impossible. I just left him in his apartment."

Reese crossed to Leatrice's husband and put a hand on his shoulder. "I need to talk to you about that conversation."

"I'm telling you, my Honeybun would never kill anyone," Leatrice said. "Even for me. He might look like a tough alpha type, but he wouldn't hurt anyone."

Kate gave me a look that told me she'd never exactly considered Sidney Allen an alpha, but neither of us said anything.

Sidney Allen's eyes widened, and he swiped at his upper lip.
"You can't think I had anything to do with someone's death."

"You did threaten him," Richard muttered loud enough for
us all to hear.

Leatrice sank down onto the sofa and dabbed at her nose.
"This is all my fault. If only I'd gotten better disguises, he never
would have made me."

"Not the takeaway I was expecting," Kate said.

"I'm not accusing you of anything." Reese used his most
patient tone of voice. "But I do need to establish a time line of
everyone who entered Mr. Kopchek's apartment or interacted
with him."

"Just because an old man died?" Alton asked. "He probably
had a heart attack. He looked like he was at least seventy."

Leatrice stifled a cry, and Hermès jumped into her lap, his
tail wagging.

"I don't think he had a heart attack," my husband admitted
with a heavy breath. "I suspect he was murdered."

Sidney Allen slapped a hand over his mouth moments before
his eyes rolled up into the back of his head, and he slumped to
the floor.

"Goodness." Richard eyed the entertainment diva sprawled
on the floor as Leatrice and Hermès both ran to his side. "That
was a bit dramatic, n'est-ce pas?"

CHAPTER SEVEN

"It's a good thing I'm cooking something that can hold," Richard grumbled when I joined him in the kitchen.

The stockpot on the stove was uncovered, and the savory smell of stew mixed with the sweetness of the bubbling mulling spices. My stomach growled, reminding me that it had been a while since lunch. "You do know there's been a possible murder in the building, right?"

Richard flicked his gaze to mine. "At this point, what are the chances you wouldn't stumble over a dead body? I've learned not to be shocked by murder at the most inopportune times."

I hated to admit that he had a point. Dead bodies did have a way of popping up when we least needed them.

"At least Sidney Allen isn't hurt." I peeked over the divider into the living room to where the entertainment coordinator was stretched out across the length of the yellow twill couch. Leatrice knelt next to him holding a cold compress to his forehead.

"Of course, he's not hurt. He had plenty of padding to catch his fall." He touched a hand to his flat stomach encased in a

Santa apron. "Unlike some of us, who would bruise like a peach."

"Be nice." I gave Richard a stern look, or at least my best attempt at one. "He's had a big shock."

Richard shrugged. "Maybe."

"What does that mean?"

Richard leveled his wooden spoon at me and lowered his voice, casting a furtive glance toward the living room. "Has it ever occurred to you, darling, that Sidney Allen may, in fact, be a diabolical killer?"

I stared at him. "Sidney Allen? The man who gives his performers code names and falls to pieces if the vendor meals aren't up to his standards?"

"Exactly. He's so high-strung that it makes total sense he would lose his temper and kill someone in a fit of rage."

I shook my head. "There's a difference between being a drama queen and being a murderer."

Richard put one hand on his hip. "Is there?"

Hermès chose that moment to scamper into the room in his designer dog sweater, circle Richard's feet a few times, and run back out.

"For your sake, you'd better hope so," I muttered.

Richard spun back to face the stove. "I heard that, Annabelle. If you're comparing me to Sidney Allen, you can bite your tongue. I am *nothing* like him."

I opened one of the cabinets and found a glass, pressing it to the automatic water dispenser in the door of the refrigerator. "I actually came in here to get some water for him, and to ask you to hold dinner until after Reese has finished his questioning."

"At least someone is treating him like the suspect he is," Richard said, with another flourish of his spoon. "We really are lucky you nabbed a police detective considering your talent for attracting crime."

I sighed as I walked back out to the living room, handing the water to Leatrice. Sidney Allen was propped up on a pile of cushions, his face still pale but his eyes open. Kate sat in one of the chairs across from the couch, while Fern was chatting with Alton by the windows. Even from a distance, I could see that the snow fell in sheets outside.

My husband sat on the coffee table, his elbows on his knees as he leaned forward. "Why don't you tell me what happened? From the beginning."

Sidney Allen nodded, taking a small sip of the water Leatrice held to his lips. "Like I said earlier, I was just getting home from a stressful afternoon. The hotel called to cancel the event, but my performers were already on-site, which meant I still needed to pay them. Plus, with the snow coming down so hard, some of them couldn't leave, so I had an entire flock of sugarplum fairies camped out in the lobby."

Leatrice dabbed at his forehead with the cold cloth. "You poor dear."

"I didn't know a group of fairies was called a flock," Kate said. "You learn something new every day."

"So, you were upset when you came into the building," Reese prodded.

"Very." Sidney Allen shifted on the pillows. "All I wanted to do was collapse on the couch and put my feet up."

"Mission accomplished," Richard said from the kitchen, gaining him a swift glare from me.

Sidney Allen either hadn't heard Richard, or more likely, chose to pretend he hadn't heard him. "I hadn't even reached my apartment door when Mr. Kopchek came stomping down the stairs."

"So, he was inside the building?" my husband asked. "He wasn't just coming inside like you?"

Sidney Allen frowned for a moment, as if in thought. "No, he was definitely inside. He wasn't wearing a coat, and he walked down from the second floor."

Leatrice put a hand to her mouth. "He must have been waiting for you."

"What happened next?" my husband asked.

"He was pretty upset—ranting and raving about Leatrice being a menace to the building." Sidney Allen's cheeks flushed. "He said some awful things."

"That must have made you angry," Reese said.

"Naturally." Sidney Allen sat up straighter on the mound of cushions. "I tried to defend my Honeybun, but he wouldn't stop saying he was going to press charges and have her arrested."

Leatrice's face was grim, and her gaze dropped to the floor.

"Was that when you threatened him?" Reese's voice was calm and soothing, reminding me that he was practiced at getting information from suspects, and that Sidney Allen was still a suspect.

The man bobbed his head up and down. "But I didn't mean it. I was just tired and angry, and he wouldn't stop threatening my wife."

"Understandable," Reese said. "How did he react when you threatened him?"

Sidney Allen's face was mottled with patches of pink as he drew in a breath. "He said something about not being afraid of either of us."

Leatrice's head snapped up. "Why would he be afraid of me?"

"Because you stalked him?" Kate said from behind her hand as she pretended to cough.

Reese didn't turn, although I saw the corner of his mouth quiver. "Did he say anything else?"

Sidney Allen rubbed a hand across his forehead. "Not then. He stomped up to his apartment, and I came to find Leatrice after realizing she wasn't in our place."

"But when you left here, you went to apologize to Mr. Kopchek?"

"I had to," Sidney Allen said. "I'd been in the wrong."

My husband rested his chin on his entwined hands. "How did that go?"

"I knocked on his door, and he opened it. I apologized for my actions and also told him that my wife was sorry for bothering him." Sidney Allen shot a look at Leatrice. "I promised him that she would stop."

"How did he respond?" Reese asked.

"Better than I expected, but he was in the middle of eating, so maybe he was eager to be rid of me. He did seem distracted and less energetic than earlier."

My husband leaned forward. "How so?"

Sidney Allen shrugged. "He kept coughing for one. He said a bite of pizza must have gone down the wrong way, so I let him go so he could get some water."

"And that was it?" Reese leaned back, resting his hands on his knees.

"That was it. I continued down to our apartment, where I stayed until I came back up here and heard you all talking about Mr. Kopchek dying."

"Did he close the door after you?"

"I don't remember. I'm pretty sure I walked away before then, so I can't be sure if it was shut all the way or not."

Reese put a hand on Sidney Allen's shoulder as he stood. "Thanks for talking to me. This has been helpful."

I followed my husband as he walked from the living room and ducked into the kitchen. "Was it helpful?"

He nodded. "I don't think Sidney Allen killed the man if that's what you're asking."

"Don't go rushing to conclusions, Detective," Richard said, the disappointment clear on his face.

"Why not?" I asked, then held up a hand before Richard could interject. "*Not* that I think Sidney Allen is guilty."

"The way Sidney Allen described the man when he answered the door makes me think there's a solid chance he'd already ingested poison. Not to mention the fact that his skin was slightly yellow when we found the body. Of course, I'll need a tox screening to be sure."

"Poison?" Richard put a hand to his throat. "Do not say that word."

My best friend did not have a great track record with poison cases. He usually ended up being a suspect, and a caterer being suspected of poisoning was never good for business.

"It could also have been an allergic reaction, but I didn't notice a rash," Reese said. "Unless Sidney Allen is lying and had more contact with the victim than he claims, I don't see how he could have poisoned him or introduced a deadly allergen."

I grabbed my husband's arm. "The pizza! Mr. Kopchek ordered a pizza. I saw the delivery guy on his way out. He was complaining that the old man never tipped. Sidney Allen said he was eating when he knocked on his door, and we saw the open pizza box on his kitchen counter. Could the poison have been in the pizza?"

Richard inhaled sharply. "I've heard of delivery guys being upset about bad tippers, but murder seems a bit extreme, don't you think?"

"Agreed," my husband said, making Richard puff out his chest. "Unless the pizza guy had another motive, it's a stretch to think he poisoned the man. Not that the pizza wasn't poisoned, but I would guess it was done by someone who really wanted Mr. Kopchek dead."

"Who would want to kill a little old man who lives alone?" I asked.

"That's what we have to find out," my husband said, his eyes glinting with determination. "No one kills a man in my apartment building at Christmas and gets away with it."

"I like your spirit," Richard said.

I put my hands on my hips. "When I say things like that, I'm meddling and causing trouble."

Richard picked up a pot holder and fanned himself with it, smiling at my tall, dark, and handsome husband. "When your husband says it, it has a certain je ne sais quoi, darling."

I groaned. Richard's French was not helping.

CHAPTER EIGHT

"Do you think we should be eating at a time like this?" Kate whispered to me as I handed her a bowl of stew.

I looked over the divider into the living room. Reese had gone back into my office to talk to someone at the police station, but everyone else was still gathered in the living room. Aside from Sidney Allen, who had insisted on going back down to his apartment to lie down. He'd insisted on going alone, much to Leatrice's dismay, and she sat on the couch looking distraught.

"What's the alternative?" I asked. "Everyone is starving."

She shivered. "I know, but if the man died of poisoning. . ." She glanced down at the meaty stew.

"How do you know that?" I asked. I thought only Richard and I knew what Reese suspected about the crime.

"I guessed after Richard made a point of saying that his stew was perfectly safe to eat."

I rolled my eyes. Just great. "Do you think anyone else figured it out?"

"Anyone who knows Richard."

I glanced back at the group. So almost everyone, except for

the cute bar owner who was sitting on one of the armchairs with his legs crossed casually as he tapped away on his phone.

"So," I said, my gaze fixing on my assistant, "what do you think of Alton?"

Kate shrugged without looking at him. "Not my type."

"I thought breathing was your type," Richard said as he came back into the kitchen after delivering bowls.

She made a face at him. "Hilarious." She looked pointedly at her stew. "I sure hope this is safe to eat."

Richard's pupils flared. "Are you implying—"

"She's just teasing you," I said, cutting him off, "but you pretty much told everyone that the old man might have been poisoned."

Richard squared his shoulders. "I did no such thing. I merely reassured people that it was safe to eat my food."

"Why would anyone think it wasn't?" I asked.

"He *has* been accused of poisoning more than once," Kate said in a stage whisper.

"You know I was set up!" Richard's voice rose to a near shriek.

I held up my hands. "Why don't we take it down a notch? We're stuck here together until the snow lets up, and there's already been one murder."

"It's the holidays from hell," Richard murmured. "I don't know how I'm going to pull off a chateau theme with all this chaos."

There was a knock on the door, and Kate and Richard both swung their heads to me.

"Are you expecting anyone else?" Richard asked. "If you invited more random guests…"

"I didn't," I said. "I can't imagine who would be here who isn't already."

Kate stirred her stew slowly as steam billowed up. "All of our friends just walk into your apartment."

Before I could answer the door, Fern had crossed the room and flung it open. It took me a moment to place the couple standing in the doorway.

"Hey Mindy," I called as I hurried out of the kitchen. "Did you guys get your heating cranked up again?"

The couple looked a bit startled to see so many people crowded into my living room.

"We did," Kurt said finally, giving me a weak grin as I waved them inside.

Mindy followed him, but her foot caught on one of the bags still gathered near the door and she pitched forward, Kurt catching her elbow at the last minute.

I shoved a duffel bag closer to the wall. "I'm so sorry about that. We haven't taken our bags back yet."

"We haven't unpacked either," Kurt said. "Wishful thinking that we'll be able to reschedule our flight I guess."

"So, you live in the building?" Fern asked.

They both nodded, and he sagged visibly, pressing a hand to his heart.

"I thought they were one of your wedding couples, sweetie," he whispered to me. "I was very worried for you."

Mindy laughed. "I wish we could use Annabelle, but we're getting married at Kurt's family's house in Newport."

Fern's eyebrows lifted, and he appraised Mindy's hair. "Well, if you need a hairstylist, sweetie, I do travel."

She laughed as he sauntered away. "Doesn't he have a salon nearby?"

"Yes, but his passion is weddings." I decided not to mention that he often dressed to match the bridesmaids and had a penchant for doing extravagant bridal hair. "But you didn't come up here looking for a hairstylist. What can I do for you two?"

"We hate to impose," Mindy said, "but do you happen to have any cream?"

Kurt put an arm around Mindy's shoulders. "Since we're snowed in, Mindy is trying to pull together some sort of dinner."

"I've got all the ingredients for my mother's pumpkin chiffon pie except for heavy cream."

I turned to ask Richard, but he was already heading for us with a small paper carton in his hand.

"If you're anything like me," he said, with a wink, "you go through enough cream at the holidays to float a boat."

I would have been surprised by Richard's warm reception of the couple, but Mindy did have a choker of pearls around her neck and wore what appeared to be a pink cashmere sweater. The combination was kryptonite to Richard's snark.

Mindy let out a sigh and beamed at him. "This will be a pared-down Christmas, but I wanted to at least have my mother's traditional pie. Thank you so much."

Richard winked at her. "You can thank me by sharing that pie recipe."

Mindy laughed again, apparently not knowing how serious Richard was.

I nudged Richard as he stared pointedly at her then turned back to the couple. "We're having a casual dinner. Why don't you join us?"

"We couldn't," Mindy said. "We wouldn't want to impose on you and your friends."

"It isn't just friends," Richard said. "One of your other neighbors is here."

Mindy and Kurt glanced at Alton, and Kurt waved in greeting. "That's the guy who owns the bar by the water, right?"

"The Salty Dog," Richard said, his nose wrinkling, either in displeasure at the name or the bar itself.

"We've never been," Mindy said, sharing an expression similar to Richard's. "I don't even think I've noticed him in the building."

"He comes in late," I said. "Bar hours."

"We're nine-to-five people," Kurt said. "Not too many late nights anymore."

"I do know *her*." Mindy's gaze landed on Leatrice. "She used to follow me. Doesn't she have a little dog?"

"That's my dog." Richard frowned. "She only babysits."

"And she's harmless," I said. "You sure you don't want to join us?"

Kurt hesitated. "It does smell good."

Richard smiled. "Of course, it does. It's beef bourguignon, or I should say, bœuf bourguignon."

Mindy put a hand on Kurt's arm. "Why don't you start eating, and I'll run this cream down and get the pie in the oven. Then we can all have pie for dessert."

Richard clapped his hands together. "Wonderful. I can try to guess all the ingredients, and you can tell me how close I am."

"Okay," Mindy said, looking a bit confused.

"It's a game he likes to play with new dishes," I told her.

"I'll be right back," she said, slipping out of the door as Richard pulled Kurt toward the kitchen.

"What happened to there being too many people to feed?" Kate asked as she walked up to me, passing Richard and Kurt.

"The guy told him it smelled great," I said. "You know Richard is a softie with anyone who compliments his food."

Kate took a bite of her stew and moaned softly. "It is pretty delicious."

I glanced around the room, realizing that everyone was eating, and I'd left my bowl in the kitchen. I headed back but stopped in the hallway when I saw my husband emerge from my office. Even though the savory scent beckoned me, I walked past the kitchen and met him in the middle of the hall.

"Were you able to reach anyone at the police station?" I asked.

"Hobbes was still at District Two, but he doesn't know how

fast the medical examiner will be able to get here." He laced his fingers with mine and walked with me toward the kitchen.

"Like you thought," I said, then I realized something that made me cringe. "You don't think the body will start smelling before they can get it out, do you?"

"In this weather and with the dodgy heaters in this building? Not a chance."

I let out a breath. It was one thing to know that there was a dead body a couple of floors down. It was quite another thing to smell it.

"Body?" Kurt asked, his spoon frozen halfway to his lips as he stepped out of the kitchen.

I'd forgotten that we hadn't mentioned the death of Mr. Kopchek to the couple. "Sorry we forgot to tell you. Your neighbor Mr. Kopchek died earlier."

"Died? The old man who lives on our floor?"

"Unfortunately. Did you know him well?"

Kurt shook his head slowly. "Not at all. We didn't even see him much."

"Didn't he complain about your bike being in the hall?" I asked.

He rolled his eyes. "I didn't take that too seriously. Besides, it's not like the bike is blocking anything since it's tucked away on the ground floor. I think he was a lonely old guy who liked to complain."

That sounded about right.

"Did you see him at all today?" my husband asked. His tone was light, but I knew he was asking because he was gathering evidence and information.

Kurt frowned as he thought. "No." He pointed his spoon at me. "You saw us running back in from our failed attempt at getting to the airport. We went straight to our apartment and then came up here to borrow the cream." He shifted his gaze to my husband. "So, what happens to the old guy now?"

"Even in a blizzard, bodies need to be processed and removed."

"Hear, hear," Richard muttered.

Reese managed a grin. "My partner is on his way, but who knows how long that will take."

"I thought Hobbes was traveling for the holidays," I said, remembering that Hobbes was supposed to visit our friend and cake designer Alexandra in Scotland. The oddly matched couple had been dating for a while and managed to make a distance relationship work. Part of me suspected that Hobbes wasn't the only man that the exotic cake designer was dating, but that might have been my reluctance to believe someone as glamorous as she would date a slightly doughy guy with a comb-over.

My husband slipped an arm around my waist. "I don't think anyone is traveling from D.C. anymore."

"Or around it," I added.

"We made it!"

The booming voice from the front door made us both turn as our friends Buster and Mack staggered inside.

"I can't believe they're here," I said. Their floral shop was several blocks away, including a steep hill, and I knew they hadn't ridden their Harleys through the blizzard. Since traffic was at a standstill and the roads virtually impassable, that meant they'd walked.

Reese gaped at the burly men in their usual head-to-toe black as they stomped their motorcycle boots on the floor. "I can't believe they're still wearing leather."

CHAPTER NINE

I helped Mack out of his cold, stiff motorcycle jacket, ignoring the melted snow dripping off him and onto my hardwood floors. "You're lucky you're not frozen."

Tiny ice crystals still dotted his dark red goatee, and he rubbed his thick arms briskly. "It wasn't so bad. No one else is out on the sidewalks."

"You're lucky you could find the sidewalks," my husband said.

Buster gave a low laugh as he adjusted the motorcycle goggles that sat on top of his bald head, and water dripped down his face. "We did lose them a time or two."

"Tell me again why you trudged through a blizzard to get here?" Richard asked, thrusting two bowls of stew at them. "For all you know, we could have already left for the holidays."

Mack lowered his nose to the bowl and inhaled deeply. "Kate texted us to say you were all stuck."

"Then Prue called us to say she was stuck at her friend's house with Merry and they were staying over there." Buster lumbered over to the couch and sat down, his leather making a painful groaning sound.

"We decided to join you all instead of staying at the flower shop," Mack said. "Despite all our holiday decor, it's not very cheery with just the two of us."

Kate threw her warms open wide. "The more the merrier."

"Says someone not involved in the meal planning," Richard said, pivoting on his heel and heading back to the kitchen.

"Ignore him," Kate whispered. "He's just in a mood because of the poisoning."

Reese shook his head but didn't say anything. It was impossible to unring that bell.

Both men paused with their spoons in midair. "Poisoning?"

"Not here," I told them. "Well, not *here* here. One of our neighbors died, and Reese suspects foul play."

"We're still waiting for a ME to make an official assessment," my husband said, glancing down at his phone.

Mack's spoon fell from his hand and splattered droplets of stew into his face. "Did this neighbor eat stew?"

"No, pizza," Leatrice said. "It's too bad he died, and we didn't get the chance to invite him to join us. I'll bet he would have appreciated a home-cooked meal. Especially after the run-in he had with my Cupcake."

Buster gaped at her. "It sounds like we missed a lot."

"You know a Wedding Belles event," Fern said, smoothing his hair with one hand.

"Hey!" Kate and I both said in protest.

Kurt stood as Richard reappeared with a basket of crusty bread slices. "Thanks so much for the stew, but I should probably check on Mindy. I'm sure she got caught up in baking."

"You can't rush a good piecrust," Richard said, putting the basket on the coffee table.

"I should go, too." Alton stood. "I need to make sure my tropical fish aren't too cold. Thanks for the dinner and the company."

"Tropical fish." Fern drummed his fingers across his jaw. "How exotic."

The bar owner shrugged. "It's mostly a lot of upkeep, especially for the exotic species."

Both men thanked us again and left.

"You never do know about people, do you?" Fern asked, once the door had closed behind them. "Who would have thought a bar owner with tattoos would be into fish?"

"It's nice to get to know our neighbors more," Leatrice said, picking a piece of bread from the basket. "Naturally, I know their basic comings and goings, but I've never chatted with most of them before."

Kate caught my eye, and I knew we were both jealous of the neighbors who weren't subjected to Leatrice's often intense attentions.

"Speaking of our neighbors," my husband said, pulling over one of the dining room chairs to sit in. "What else do we know about the guy who owns the bar and the couple?"

"Not much." I eyed the quickly dwindling bread basket as Buster and Mack both popped pieces into their mouths. "Kate and I have seen Alton a few times when we're coming home late from weddings and he's rolling in from the bar."

Reese focused on Kate. "You're a good judge of character, especially with men. What do you think of the guy?"

Kate looked surprised. "Me?" She shrugged. "I guess I don't have much of an opinion. He seems nice enough."

Fern tilted his head at her. "Nice enough? Are you feeling well, sweetie?"

My assistant's cheeks flushed pink. "I don't notice everything about *all* men. The only thing I can tell you is that he isn't looking to date anyone, either."

"Since when are you not looking to date?" Richard asked.

"I'm telling you," Kate said, standing quickly. "He's not my type."

I knew for a fact that Kate had a soft spot for good- looking guys with tattoos, especially if they had a bit of a bad-boy vibe, like Alton did.

"Okay." My husband looked a bit taken aback as Kate stomped off down the hall.

"Blizzards are very stressful," Leatrice said. "I'm sure she'll feel better soon."

"Tensions do seem to be running high. We've already had a virtual brawl and a murder." Fern sighed. "I wish I'd brought my calming pheromones."

"Pheromones?" Buster asked.

Fern nodded. "They're actually cat pheromones, but I find them very soothing."

Mack choked on his bite of bread, and Buster pounded on his back.

"Why don't I go check on Kate?" I stood and followed her down the hall. As I suspected, she was sitting in the black chair in my office and spinning around in it.

"So," I said, stepping into the room and trying to avoid trampling on the favors for our upcoming New Year's Eve wedding. "What was that all about?"

Kate stopped spinning. "Sometimes I get tired of everyone assuming I'm some crazed dater."

I didn't point out that, until very recently, she had been a crazed dater. "You know they didn't mean any harm. Reese is just trying to learn more about our neighbors because they're all potential suspects."

"I know. I guess I kind of forgot that for a second." She bit the corner of her thumbnail. "Do you think your husband's mad at me?"

"Mad at you?" I laughed. "Of course not. But he does think you have unique insight into men. Usually you can tell if someone's cheating on their wife at fifty paces."

She let out a breath. "It's easier to pick apart other people's relationships than manage your own."

"No kidding." I sat down on the floor cross-legged. "Just look at me. How many weddings have I planned for other people, but my own wedding plans stressed me out?"

She grinned. "You were a mess."

"I think 'mess' might be a bit harsh, but just because we plan weddings doesn't mean we have any special skills when it comes to relationships or marriage ourselves."

"You can say that again." She leaned back in the chair. "One thing I can tell you about that engaged couple is that he's way more into her than she's into him."

I could see that. Kurt wasn't exactly heartthrob material, although he seemed nice enough.

"If you ask me," Kate said, "and your husband did, she's marrying him for his fancy house in Newport and the money I assume he has. Not that I think that nugget of insight has anything to do with the murder."

"She wouldn't be the first bride we've known to marry for money instead of love."

"It's still sad," Kate said.

"Since when did you become such a romantic?" I eyed her. "Gold diggers never used to bother you."

"I guess I'd never been in love before."

I stared at her until she looked up and met my gaze. "You're kidding me. You're in love? Like really in love?"

She gave me a thin smile. "Really, truly, miserably in love."

"Miserably?" My heart caught in my chest. "Why miserably? Is he married? Terminally ill? Does he live in Outer Mongolia?"

She choked back a laugh. "None of those."

"Then what gives?" I threw my hands into the air. "Why won't you tell me who this guy is?"

"Because it's your husband's brother," she said, her voice soft. "I'm in love with Daniel."

CHAPTER TEN

I didn't speak for a few moments. For as long as I'd known Kate, she'd never even flirted with the idea of love. Lust, sure, but love she'd seemed happy to look askance at and leave for others.

"I thought you just flirted with him like you flirt with everyone."

She ran a hand through her hair. "That's what it was at first —harmless flirting. But then he took me out a few times, and we talked a lot. He actually listened to me and wanted to know what I thought. You don't know because you barely dated before you met the detective, but men in D.C. mostly talk about themselves and their careers."

That sounded like a lot of the grooms we'd worked with, so no surprise there.

"How long have you been officially dating?" I asked.

"That's just the thing. This is different from my usual relationships. For one thing, there have been no sleepovers."

This took a minute to sink in. "So, you haven't…?"

She shook her head. "Nope. He wants to take things slow."

I thought about how long it had been since Kate had talked

about some new guy. "That is slow, but I guess it's good, right? Better that than wham-bam-thank-you-ma'am."

"I wouldn't mind a little wham bam at this point."

"But you are dating him, right?" I leaned back with my palms on the floor behind me. "And you're more than friends?"

She gave me a withering look. "I haven't lost my mojo entirely, Annabelle. We go out a few times a week, and he always picks me up and pays. *And* he's a really good kisser."

"I don't know why you're complaining. Most women would kill for a nice guy who takes them out, pays, and doesn't expect anything in return."

"I know, I know." She swiped at her eyes. "It's great, but I don't know if I can keep doing it."

"Why not? I thought you were in love with the guy."

"That's just it," she said. "I want more."

I studied her red-rimmed eyes. "As in…?"

She waved a hand at me. "What you have. The perfect husband who adores you."

I didn't bother to tell her that no one was perfect, and that my husband was incapable of getting his dirty T-shirts into the hamper. I was too stunned by her revelation.

"You want to get married? I thought you had sworn off the institution."

She shrugged. "I guess Daniel changed my mind."

"You should tell him," I said. "It is Christmas after all."

"No way." She pressed her lips together. "First of all, I'm not going to do it over text or the phone. And what if I freak him out or scare him off? He's almost forty, and he's never been married. What if he never wants to get married?"

"Trouble with a client?" Leatrice's pink-and-white head poked around the doorframe.

Kate straightened in the chair. "Annabelle and I were going over some details for our New Year's Eve wedding."

Leatrice tilted her head. "I though you two swore off doing holiday weddings."

"We did," I said, "but this is the second daughter in a family of four daughters."

"And they have a huge budget," Kate added. "Sometimes size does matter."

"You girls!" A flush crawled up Leatrice's wrinkled neck, and she swatted a hand through the air. "I'll leave you to your work, but I thought you'd want to know that the police are here. More police, that is."

I jumped up from the floor. "Really? I didn't think they could get here because of the storm."

Leatrice shrugged. "Maybe they prioritize dead bodies."

"Or maybe they prioritize dead bodies in buildings where cops live," Kate said.

That sounded more like it. I was sure my husband had some pull in the department, and a potential murder where he lived would definitely get bumped up the list.

Kate and I followed Leatrice back down the hall to the living room, but only Richard and Fern sat on the couch with Hermès stretched out between them and Buster and Mack jammed into the chairs across from them.

"Where's everyone else?" I asked.

Fern twisted his head toward us. "Your hot husband is with his cop friends. Unfortunately for us, he's the only tasty one in the bunch. That's why we stayed here."

"That's not the only reason," Richard said. "For once, I am not a suspect and am not needed to give a statement. Except to say I was in this apartment all afternoon."

"Aside from loading in all the food," I reminded him.

He fluttered a hand at me. "Of course, aside from that. But I couldn't exactly stop on the second floor and kill a complete stranger with an armload of bags."

He had a point. Most of us had no motive and scant opportunity.

Mack cocked one pierced eyebrow. "I'm still not clear about what happened to your neighbor."

"It's a bit of a long story," Kate said as Leatrice drew in a long breath, obviously preparing to go into every detail of said story.

"But the long and short of it is that our second-floor neighbor Mr. Kopchek," I started to say.

"Who Leatrice suspected of being a spy," Kate added.

"Dropped dead after Sidney Allen got into a heated argument with him and threatened murder." I looked between Buster and Mack. "Any questions?"

"Yes," they both said.

Leatrice huffed out a breath. "Really, dear. You left out all the important details and the part about my Honeybun being completely innocent."

"And the part about me calling in the culinary cavalry so we wouldn't starve to death," Richard said.

Fern smoothed his pristine hair. "Or about my death-defying walk from my salon carrying survival essentials."

"Hair products are not considered survival essentials," Richard told him with a tortured sigh.

"Different blokes for different folks," Kate said.

Buster frowned. "Isn't it strokes, not blokes?"

Kate grinned. "You say it your way; I'll say it mine."

Fern tapped his chin and smiled at Kate. "I like your version better, too, sweetie."

"Mon dieu," Richard muttered.

"I knew we should have come over earlier," Mack muttered to Buster. "Look at what we missed."

I headed for the door. "While you all fill in the details I forgot, I'm going to see what's going on downstairs."

Leatrice hurried over to me. "I should come with you. I did find the body."

She was right about that. "Fine, but we need to stay out of the way and let the police do their jobs."

We left Richard and Fern arguing about the merits of beauty over food, closing the door behind us. Even from two floors away, deep voices drifted up to us. I recognized the sound of my husband and his partner, Hobbes, as well as the crackling of radios. Leatrice and I walked down the stairs without talking.

When we reached the second floor, a uniformed officer was standing in front of Mr. Kopchek's door unspooling yellow police tape. He glanced up at us and frowned. "This floor is off-limits, ladies."

"We're here to see Detective Reese," I said. "I'm his wife."

He nodded, his gaze sliding to Leatrice and widening as he took in her Christmas tree camo dress and slippers that looked like wrapped presents. "And her?"

"She's a witness," I said. "She found the body."

"Mike," the officer called into the apartment, "your wife's here."

I tried not to let out an irritated sigh. The way he'd said it made me sound like a meddling nuisance.

My husband appeared in the open doorway. He wore latex gloves and the intense expression he got when he worked cases. My heart fluttered a little at the sight of him in his element.

"Hey, babe. What's up?"

For a second, the question stumped me. Why were we there? I was so used to being involved in criminal cases, I'd almost forgotten I needed a reason to insert myself into a police investigation—a detail my husband had made a point of reminding me about often in the past.

"We thought you might need Leatrice to give an official statement," I said, regaining my confidence. "Since she found the body."

He seemed about to shoot me down, then he thought better of it. "Actually, I do want her to take a look at the crime scene and make sure it's like she remembered it when she first found the deceased." He waved us forward. "But put on booties and don't touch a thing."

Leatrice and I both put plastic booties over our shoes—they barely stretched over Leatrice's oversized slippers—and followed him inside the apartment again. The pungent smell of pepperoni had faded, and my nose twitched from the telltale scent of death. I put a hand over my mouth, the bitter tang of bile tickling the back of my throat.

We walked down the short entry hall, passing the kitchen where a photographer was taking pictures of the open pizza box. In the living room, a woman wearing the same gloves as my husband was now huddled beside the body, and Detective Hobbes stood next to her in a tan blazer that strained over his belly.

Leatrice swiveled her head around the room. "Aside from all the extra people, it looks the same."

I darted a glance at Mr. Kopchek, still slumped over. The pizza on his TV tray looked cold, the cheese congealed over the lip of the plate, and a lump formed in my throat at the sad, lonely sight.

My husband nodded. "Let's go back outside, and you can give me your official statement."

As we turned to go, I stopped, my heart beating faster. "Wait. Something's different." I scanned the room again as my brain tried to replay when I'd first seen the body. I pointed to the TV tray. "There was a mug next to that plate. Where's his mug?"

CHAPTER ELEVEN

"You're sure?" Detective Hobbes asked me as we stood gathered outside Mr. Kopchek's apartment.

My husband was inside the apartment, searching fruitlessly for the mug we both knew was gone. Even the ring of condensation on the TV tray belied its absence and proved that it had been removed in a hurry.

I wrapped my arms around myself. The halls in the building weren't heated, and the gusts of icy air from the arriving police officers and medical examiner had made the stairwell cold enough for me to see the puff of my breath. "Positive. It had some sort of corporate logo on it. I didn't look close enough to notice what it said, but it was one of those basic, white mugs with a logo printed on the side in blue."

Hobbes scribbled in his notebook. "Any clue what was in it?"

"I didn't notice."

"Neither did I," Leatrice added. "Actually, I didn't notice the mug at all. I was too distracted by poor Mr. Kopchek."

Hobbes nodded without looking up. "It might have been empty by the time you saw it."

"You think that's what killed him, don't you?" Leatrice spoke in a hush. "Someone poisoned his drink?"

Hobbes glanced up at us then looked right back down without answering. My husband came out of the apartment, shaking his head.

"No luck?" I asked, although I knew the mug hadn't hidden itself, and none of the officers were foolish enough to move something at a crime scene.

"Clearly, the scene of the crime wasn't as secure as I thought it was." His forehead was furrowed in deep creases.

"But you closed the door when we left," Leatrice said. "I saw you take the key and pull the door closed."

"And all these doors lock automatically when you shut them," I said, remembering that because of this quirk, I'd locked myself out of my apartment more than once. That is until I'd had to have the locks replaced and the locksmith had installed a door that didn't automatically lock—at Kate's request since she'd gotten tired of us getting locked out and having to tramp down to get Leatrice's spare key.

Leatrice snapped her fingers, bouncing on the toes of her slippers and making the bows on them bobble. "What if someone else in the building has a key? I have a copy of your key and you two have one of mine."

Reese flicked his gaze to me. Leatrice had a key to our apartment because she'd made one using her secret agent key impression kit.

"Did *you* have a copy of Mr. Kopchek's key?" I asked her.

She gave me a look of total innocence. "Why would I have a key, dear? We barely did more than exchange greetings."

I wanted to remind her that she had been following him, but I let it go for the moment. "Mr. Kopchek didn't seem like the type to exchange keys with neighbors."

"Agreed," my husband said, looking at the floor in front of the door. "And there's no mat to hide one under." His gaze went to the only other apartment on the second floor. "I guess if he wanted anyone to have a key, it would be the people right next door."

I followed his line of sight. I wasn't so sure about that. "Kurt said they barely knew the guy. Leatrice aside, this isn't a very social building."

"I'd still like to check with them." My husband took a few long steps to the closed wooden door and rapped on it a few times.

After a beat, the door swung open. Mindy stood in the doorway, her hair pulled up into a messy ponytail. Her pink cashmere sweater had been replaced with a long-sleeved T-shirt and the sleeves were pushed up. The scent of pumpkin wafted past her and into the hall. I guessed the pie baking was going well.

She looked at my husband then past him to the commotion in the hall. "You're the cop who lives upstairs, right?"

My husband held out his hand. "Detective Mike Reese."

"Kurt told me about Mr. Kopchek." She shook her head. "So sad."

"Kurt also told us you didn't know him very well," Reese said.

"That's right." She crossed her arms over her chest. "He wasn't what you'd call chatty. He didn't mind leaving notes, but he wasn't into pleasantries."

"Did you get citations?" I asked, ignoring my husband's sharp glance.

Mindy twitched one shoulder. "I think everyone did. He didn't like the way I parked out front. He said I went over the line into the no-parking zone. As if everyone in Georgetown doesn't creep over the line. Plus, he hated that Kurt kept his bike in the downstairs hall."

"I've gotten those parking notes, too," I said. "I'm surprised my assistant, Kate, hasn't had her car papered with them. She's actually a terrible parker."

Mindy smiled. "I ignored them. It's not like they were actual tickets."

"I take it you and Mr. Kopchek didn't exchange keys then?" my husband asked, obviously trying to steer the conversation away from complaining about Mr. Kopchek's citations.

Mindy snorted out a laugh. "Exchange keys? He barely said hello when we passed in the hall."

"So that's a no?" Reese asked.

"That's a no," she said.

"You don't happen to have any copies of the citations he gave out, do you?" my husband asked. "Just for the file."

"I throw them out as soon as I get them. They never even make it up here." She twisted her head and looked behind her. "Maybe Kurt has one. Kurt, honey, do you have a copy of one of Mr. Kopchek's notes?"

Kurt appeared behind her. "About my bike? Maybe." He dug in the pockets of one of the coats hanging on the wall by the door, pulling out a crumpled piece of paper. "Here's one."

He handed it to Reese, who uncrumpled and scanned the paper. I didn't need to peer over his shoulder since I'd seen the printed citations enough times myself.

"Did these tickets create any bad blood between you and the victim?" My husband asked the couple.

Kurt looked shocked. "Bad blood? Just because he left weird notes? No way. We just laughed it off and thought he was a little nutty."

Mindy's gaze traveled to Leatrice, taking in her outfit and hair. "Georgetown is filled with eccentric types."

"I know you came in this evening after the storm started. Did you see Mr. Kopchek at any time?" Reese asked.

"Not today," Kurt answered for both of them. "We were in a rush to get out of here, then when we came home, we came straight up here. Your wife held the door open for us."

"That was when we were carrying in all the food," I said.

"Was Mr. Kopchek's door closed when you came home?" Reese asked.

Kurt paused before answering. "Definitely. Right, hon?"

"As far as I remember," she said. "It wasn't standing open."

"You must have heard me screaming when I found him," Leatrice said. "You would have been home by then."

The couple had blank looks on their faces.

"Sorry," Mindy said. "Kurt had some holiday music playing, and you know how thick these old doors are."

We hadn't heard Leatrice screaming either, but we were two floors up.

"Why all the questions?" Kurt asked.

Reese gave his own half shrug. "Trying to determine when he died and cause of death."

"It wasn't old age?" Mindy asked. "He looked pretty old."

Leatrice bristled beside me. Mr. Kopchek had looked significantly younger than she did.

"I can't say." My husband shook both their hands. "Ongoing investigation. Thanks for answering my questions."

After they'd closed the door, he turned around. "So much for them having a key."

"I'm telling you, he wasn't the kind of guy to swap keys," I said, pointing to the citation in his hand. "He gave his neighbors tickets, for heaven's sake."

"Then if there wasn't a second key, how did someone get inside the apartment I locked?" He narrowed his eyes at Mr. Kopchek's door, then angled his head. "Unless..." Hurrying to the door, he pulled the latex gloves out of his pocket and snapped them on again, kneeling down and inspecting the locking mechanism. When he stood, he blew out a breath.

"Well...?" I asked.

"My hunch was right," he said. "There are traces of some sort of sticky residue on the door's strike plate and locking mechanism."

"Residue?"

Leatrice sucked in a breath. "Someone put tape on it to keep it from locking."

"So, it didn't matter that we closed the door." Chills went through me that had nothing to do with the cold. "Whoever used the tape could go back inside anyway to remove the mug."

My husband gave me a grim smile. "And they removed the tape after they left so the door would be locked when the police arrived."

"Someone did kill Mr. Kopchek," I whispered. "And returned to remove the evidence, which means the killer was someone who had access between the time we first saw the body and when the police arrived."

"That clears me." Leatrice put the back of her hand to her forehead.

I thought back to everyone who'd been in my apartment and when they'd left. "But it doesn't clear Sidney Allen."

CHAPTER TWELVE

"You don't think my Cupcake would murder someone, do you?" Leatrice looked at me like I'd sprouted a second head.

Even though I had seen Sidney Allen lose his temper at events before, I had a hard time imagining the man actually killing someone. Besides, poison was a premeditated method, and Sidney Allen was definitely a heat-of-the-moment type of person. Not that I wanted to think about the passionate nature of an elderly man with the physique of Humpty Dumpty.

"No," I assured Leatrice, reaching for her bony hand. "My point is that we should make a list of anyone who could have possibly gone into the apartment after we locked it—or thought we did."

"That's easy." Leatrice held up her other hand and started counting off fingers. "After we returned to your apartment, the only people who left were the cute bar owner and my Honeybun."

"But there were other people who were moving around the building," my husband said. "The couple we just talked to, for instance. And Buster and Mack."

"Buster and Mack?" My voice went up a few octaves, and the

officer stretching police tape across the staircase bannister looked over. "They didn't even know the man or that he was dead."

"I know that," Reese said, his voice irritatingly even. "But if we're really considering all possibilities, we have to add them to the mix. They did have opportunity to enter the apartment after we left it."

"But they weren't here earlier." Leatrice wagged a finger at him. "So, they couldn't have been the ones to kill him."

"That's a good point," Reese said. "That brings us back to the couple in 2A, the bar owner, and Sidney Allen. Unless there are other people in the building we haven't seen."

Leatrice shook her head, and her flipped-up hairdo swung around her face like a bell. "Both 3B and 4A left yesterday for the holidays."

There was no point in asking how she knew or if she was certain. I don't think Reese or I wanted to know the answers.

"We can't discount the possibility that Mr. Kopchek let his killer into the building, and it isn't someone who lives here," my husband said.

Leatrice shivered. "It does make more sense. Aside from being annoyed at his notes, why would anyone in the building have a reason to kill him? No one knew him."

"So, he buzzes someone in, the person kills him, leaves, and then comes back to take the mug with the poison?" I made a face. "Why not just take the mug right away? Why did the killer need to come back for it? And where would someone who didn't live here go between those two time frames? It's a blizzard outside. It's not like our stairwell has any places to hide. And people were walking up and down it, so anyone trying to hide would have been seen."

"She makes good points, Detective," Leatrice said, her head swinging back to him.

Reese gave me a smile, his hazel eyes locking on mine. "She usually does."

I returned his smile, arching an eyebrow. "What can I say? I'm married to a cop."

Hobbes cleared his throat as he walked out of the apartment and joined us. "Got some preliminary findings."

"Was I right?" my husband asked him. "Does the ME also think it's poison?"

Hobbes glanced at us quickly, but apparently gave up any thought of keeping the conversation private. "She won't know until the toxicology results come back, and that could take a while all things considered, but she agrees the victim's skin and swollen airways indicate poison."

Reese's eyes danced. "Not an allergic reaction?"

"Nope. No rash. She suspects some sort of chemical. Could be a household product or something more industrial."

My husband looked pleased that his initial assessment had been spot-on. "Because the coffee mug was missing, it's a good guess that the victim drank it. Now we just need to figure out what poison was used and who had the motive to give it to him."

Hobbes rubbed a hand across his wrinkled forehead, not looking nearly as satisfied. "We definitely have another murder on our hands."

I rubbed my arms briskly, chilled by both the cold air and the thought that someone gave an old man some sort of household or industrial poison. "I know it's poison, but it seems like a pretty violent way to kill someone."

"It wouldn't have been a fun way to go," Hobbes said. "But it would have been pretty fast. Five or ten minutes depending on how much he ingested."

"That poor man," Leatrice murmured.

"So, what next?" I asked my husband. "We don't have many suspects, and we have zero motives so far."

His partner eyed me. "We?"

I remembered too late that my husband's partner had never warmed to the idea of me and my friends getting involved with murder investigations. To be fair, Reese hadn't so much warmed to the idea as given in to the inevitable. He knew I had an uncontrollable need to fix things—which included crimes that affected my clients or friends or, in this case, neighbors—so he'd learned to work my involvement into his process.

My husband slipped his blazer off and wrapped it around my shoulders. "What Annabelle means is that she's concerned one of our neighbors was killed and the possibility that another resident could be involved."

The navy wool blazer still held his body heat, and I stopped shivering almost as soon as he'd put it on me. "That's exactly what I meant. Not to mention, I have an apartment filled with potential witnesses. We still don't know what everyone saw as they came and went from the building."

"I'm supposed to be halfway to Scotland by now," Hobbes said under his breath, scowling at the floor.

"You were spending Christmas with Alexandra?" My husband had mentioned his partner's trip to me, but I didn't want it to sound like we'd been talking about him, so I pretended I didn't know.

"It was supposed to be a surprise," he said, finally meeting my eyes and shuffling his feet. "She didn't even know I was coming."

"How romantic." Leatrice pressed her hands over her heart. "I love it when my Sugar Muffin surprises me."

Knowing the exotic cake designer, I wasn't so sure. She didn't strike me as the type who liked having a visit sprung on her, but maybe Hobbes knew her better. Even though I didn't understand the relationship, I'd long since given up unraveling the secrets of the heart. I'd had too many couples whose match-up baffled me to harbor any misconception that love was something easily understood.

"Maybe the storm will clear, and you can get over for New Year's," I suggested.

"Maybe." He let out a tortured breath. "For now, Mike's right. We've got witnesses to question and a bunch of paperwork to file."

My husband clapped a hand on his partner's shoulder. "Let's start upstairs. Annabelle's best friend has cooked up an amazing stew. You can eat while we work." He glanced over his shoulder at the uniformed officer by the door. "You can secure the scene for us after the ME leaves, right?"

The officer jerked his head up slightly. "You got it, Mike."

"It may not be how you planned to spend the holidays," I told Hobbes, "but we do have plenty of food and booze."

He managed a smile. "Thanks. Dinner would be good. All I've eaten today has come from a vending machine."

Leatrice waved for him to follow her as she started up the stairs. "Then you're in for a treat. Richard may be a bit of a diva, but you can't beat his food."

I thought it was bold for Leatrice to call anyone a diva considering who she'd married, but I held my tongue. When we reached the fourth floor, Leatrice opened the door and waved Detective Hobbes in. The warm air hit me immediately, as did the savory scent of stew mixed with the sweet aroma of cinnamon and something else I couldn't identify.

"You're a duck!" Richard yelled as Fern pranced around the living room with his lips pursed and his rear end sticking out.

Fern straightened and put his hands on his hips with a flourish. "A duck? I'm clearly a Kardashian."

"Should I be worried that someone slipped something in our guests' drinks?" my husband whispered as he came up behind me.

I cast my gaze over my friends. "If only."

CHAPTER THIRTEEN

"We're playing charades," Fern said when he noticed us staring. "What's Christmas without some games, right?"

"We're trying to take everyone's minds off the dead guy downstairs." Kate waved a hand at Hobbes. "Hi, Detective. Welcome to the party."

"I wouldn't call it a party," Richard said, his attention focused on Hermès as the little dog nosed around the bottom of the Christmas tree, sniffing at the remaining wrapped presents and bumping the low fir branches so that ornaments jingled.

"Why not?" Kate lifted a glass filled with crimson liquid into the air. "We have a signature cocktail."

Fern bobbed his head up and down, his grin wide as he picked up his glass from a side table. "The Blizzitini. But be warned, it has a bit of a kick."

"You wouldn't happen to have any more of your delicious stew, would you?" Reese asked Richard. "I promised my partner some dinner while we talked to witnesses."

Richard popped up from the couch. "You're in luck. I have beef bourguignon, and my gingerbread madeleines are almost ready to come out of the oven."

"You made cookies?" I asked. "How long were we downstairs anyway?"

He made an impatient face at me as he bustled by me to the kitchen. "The dough was premade in my catering kitchens. All I had to do was put it in the molds."

I inhaled again. Gingerbread. That was the scent I hadn't been able to place.

"You all really are set to ride out the storm," Hobbes said, his eyes still wide.

"Welcome to the chateau," Richard said with a dramatic flourish of his arm.

Hobbes looked confused, but my husband motioned for his partner to follow him, and they disappeared into the kitchen with Richard muttering in French behind them.

"Annabelle," Mack said, his rumble of a voice low. "What's this about witnesses? Did someone see the murder take place?"

I shook my head. "Doubtful, but the detectives want to talk to anyone who was up and down the stairs in the past couple of hours."

"Meaning us?" Mack glanced at Buster. "They don't think we had anything to do with it, do they?"

"Don't be silly," Kate said before I could answer. "Why would either of you kill an old man you didn't know."

Mack looked scandalized. "Or kill anyone?"

"Exodus 20:13," Buster said. "Thou shalt not kill."

Aside from being former members of a tough Harley-Davidson motorcycle club, our florist friends had become born-again Christians. They were members of the Biker Baptist Church and the Road Riders for Jesus, and they never cursed, much less committed murder.

"Why would *anyone* want to kill Mr. Kopchek?" I said, perching on the arm of my yellow twill couch. "I can't believe his citations were enough to drive someone to murder."

What I didn't say aloud was that if our neighbors hadn't

killed Leatrice yet, and she had been known to follow them in disguise, then why would they kill an old man who didn't do anything but issue benign complaints?

"There must have been another reason," Leatrice said as she took the place Richard vacated on the couch. "Maybe he had some skeletons in his closet or a secret dangerous past."

"Who doesn't have a few skeletons?" Fern asked, taking another sip of his drink. "But it would have to be something pretty bad to be killed over."

"What do we know about the old man?" I directed my question at Leatrice.

After a moment, she pointed to herself. "Me? You think I know dirt on Mr. Kopchek?"

"Don't you?" Kate asked, arching one eyebrow.

Leatrice hemmed and hawed for a few seconds then finally let out a loud huff. "Fine. I may have done a little background on him when he first moved in, but I do that with everyone. It's strictly a safety precaution. You can't be too safe these days. There are so many crazies out there."

Kate glanced down at Leatrice's Christmas present slippers and gave me a knowing look. Leatrice was definitely what most people would consider one of the crazies.

"I'm assuming you got help from Boots and Dapper Dan?" I said.

She gnawed at the corner of her mouth. "Please don't mention this to my Honeybun." She stole a look over her shoulder. "Or the detective. I know they don't like me working with the boys."

"The boys" were a pair of hackers she'd met on the dark web. They were skilled at getting information no one else could and staying anonymous. Leatrice had promised she would cut off all contact with them after my husband had discovered she'd used them to hack into the D.C. police department computers and had blown a gasket. As I'd suspected, she hadn't been able to cut the cord yet.

"What did you find out?" I asked, making a point not to make any promises of secrecy. I'd learned not to keep things from my husband, although I had no problem keeping her secret from Sidney Allen.

Leatrice lifted her palms up. "Nothing. He's pretty much what you'd expect. An old man who worked for the government for his entire career, never married, no kids."

Fern frowned. "And he ended up here leaving complaints for all his neighbors? That's sad."

"No chance he was a spy hiding here under an alias?" I asked. "Maybe he was actually in the witness relocation program and his cover got blown?"

Leatrice shook her head vigorously, and her multicolored hair swung around her face. "If there was anything like that, the boys would have discovered it."

"Discovered what?" my husband asked as he and Hobbes returned from the kitchen holding bright-red plates topped with soup bowls.

"Nothing," I said. "Leatrice didn't find out anything about Mr. Kopchek that would explain why he was murdered."

"Why would she?" Hobbes asked as he and Reese took seats at the dining table.

"Our neighbor fashions herself an amateur sleuth," my husband explained with a weary look at his partner.

Hobbes scanned the room, his gaze pausing on me and then Kate. "That seems to be catching around here."

I ignored the comment while Leatrice scowled at the straight-laced detective. "The point is, we can't figure out a motive. Someone went to a decent amount of trouble to knock him off. Why?"

"I think that's for us to figure out," Hobbes said.

"You should be grateful you have all of us here." Kate drained the last drops of her drink. "We've been instrumental in solving more cases than you know."

"That's right," Fern said, flopping down on the couch between Kate and Leatrice. "If we all put our heads together, I'm sure we can get this thing wrapped up before Santa pops down the chimney tomorrow night."

Leatrice patted his leg. "Annabelle doesn't have a chimney, dear."

Fern's face fell. "That's a problem."

Kate jerked her thumb behind her. "Don't worry. He probably uses the fire escape."

"Can we get back to the case?" I asked.

"Well, if you want to know what Buster and I saw when we walked up the staircase earlier, I can tell you there was nothing out of the ordinary," Mack said.

Buster nodded. "We were the only ones on the stairs, and nothing looked any different than it usually does."

"Did you notice the door open to apartment 2B?" my husband asked.

Buster stroked his dark brown goatee. "If it was, I didn't notice, so it probably wasn't standing open."

"To be honest, we were more concerned with getting upstairs and warming our frozen hands and feet," Mack said.

"Thanks, guys," Reese said, but I could tell he was disappointed they didn't remember more and couldn't give him a clue that might break the case open.

"What now?" I asked.

"We question more witnesses," Hobbes said. "You all aren't the only people in the building."

"Reese already talked to the couple who lives on Mr. Kopchek's floor," Leatrice said. "They're another dead end."

"But we haven't talked to the guy who runs the bar," my husband said. "He left when Kurt did."

Kate stood and walked to the counter between the kitchen

and living room where all the bottles of booze were lined up. "But he was here with all of us from the time we unloaded Richard's food until then."

"That's right," Fern said. "I talked to him for a while, and I can tell you that he might look like a bad boy, but he's harmless."

"He still might have seen something," Hobbes said, watching Kate as she mixed a drink in a highball glass.

There was a sharp knock on the door. Richard came out of the kitchen holding a plate of gingerbread men. "There can't possibly be any more people we know left in the city."

Leatrice bounded off the couch. "I'll bet it's my Honeybun. I knew he couldn't stay away from me forever."

She opened the door, but it was not her Honeybun. The uniformed officer from downstairs held a plastic evidence bag in one hand as he peered inside my apartment.

Hobbes and Reese stood quickly and crossed to the door.

"You found something?" my husband asked, his gaze locked on the bag.

The officer held it higher. "This was on the top of the victim's trash. The ME is going to take it back for testing, but I thought you'd want to see it first. It's the only bottle or container of liquid we found, so this might be what the old guy drank."

"Isn't that...?" I peeked around the detectives to get a better look at the half-sized wine bottle.

Leatrice let out a squeak. "One of the bottles of cider Sidney Allen and I gave as gifts to all the neighbors."

CHAPTER FOURTEEN

"You don't think Sidney Allen and Leatrice could really have anything to do with this, do you?" Kate asked, following me into the kitchen and carrying a stack of dirty bowls and plates.

I set my own handful of dirty dishes on the counter as I opened the dishwasher. "Of course not. We already determined that Sidney Allen isn't the type to premeditate a murder. Besides, they gave that cider out to the neighbors days ago, and he only got into an argument with Mr. Kopchek a couple of hours ago."

"So why did your hubby and his sidekick go down to talk to Sidney Allen and take Leatrice with them?"

I loaded my dishes then stepped back for Kate to do the same. "They have to follow procedure, especially since it's someone Reese knows. How would it look if he didn't question Sidney Allen and Leatrice after they found that bottle of cider?"

"I guess you're right." Kate straightened and closed the dishwasher door. "By the way, what did you give out to your neighbors since you live in a gift-giving building now?"

"She ordered bags of Christmas cookies from me," Richard said as he walked into the kitchen.

I held up my hands. "Guilty as charged. I was too crazed getting presents wrapped and details for the New Year's Eve wedding finalized."

"And you don't have the patience for Christmas cookies," Richard added.

"Not the way you do them," I said. "I can stick a Hershey's Kiss in a peanut butter cookie, but iced cookies that look like reindeer are beyond me."

"Speaking of cookies." Kate eyed the gingerbread madeleines cooling on the metal racks on the counter.

"Don't even think about it," Richard warned.

"Actually, this is perfect." I grabbed a plate with a red bow and holly leaves painted around the rim and started stacking it with cookies as Richard gaped at me.

"What are you doing?" he cried.

"Giving us a reason to visit Alton," I said.

"Alton?" He scowled at me. "You mean tattoo boy? Why do you need to visit him, and why do you need to take half of my madeleines to do it?"

I unloaded a few of the cookies, which garnered me more scowls from Richard.

"Kate and I need to talk to him because he's one of the people who could have gone into Mr. Kopchek's apartment after Reese thought he sealed it."

Now Kate's expression matched Richard's. "Shouldn't you wait and let your husband do that?"

"If I do, he won't take you with him."

"And why do I need to be a part of this cockamamie plan?" Kate asked.

I hooked an arm though hers. "Because even though you claim to have sworn off men, you're still the best judge of them I know. I want to know why you think something's off about the guy."

"I never said something was off about him," she said, then let out a sigh when I gave her a pointed look. "I do get a vibe that he's hiding something, but I'm also a bit rusty."

"I still trust your rusty instinct." I tugged her forward. "That's why we're going to talk to him. The cookies are just our excuse."

Richard glanced at his remaining cookies. "I was going to start on the Bûche de Noël, but I suppose I'd better make more madeleines."

We left Richard fussing in the kitchen and muttering in French under his breath. As we passed through the living room, I saw that Fern was mixing up more cocktails, and Buster and Mack were FaceTiming with baby Merry while Hermès yipped into the phone.

"They won't even notice we're gone," I said to Kate as we slipped out the door.

The stairwell was surprisingly quiet after the previous bustle of the police around Mr. Kopchek's apartment, and it hadn't warmed up much since they'd left. We walked down one floor, and I rapped sharply on the door I knew belonged to Alton.

After a moment, the door opened. The man had changed into gray sweatpants and a hoodie, and his feet were bare.

"We brought you some cookies," I said, trying to make my voice as cheerful as possible as I stepped forward. "You left before my friend served them, and we didn't want you to miss them. Where should I put them?"

He looked slightly startled as he stepped back and allowed us inside. "Um, anywhere is fine. Thanks for bringing them. You really didn't have to—"

"Don't mention it," I said, talking over him as I walked down the short hallway and into the main room. Alton's apartment was a similar layout to Mr. Kopchek's, which made sense. It was directly above the old man's apartment.

Instead of thick curtains and dark, dated furniture, the bar owner had bare windows and lots of glass and black leather. No shock there. He was a single guy, after all, and single men seemed to gravitate toward black leather. A large standing aquarium stood against one wall, and a wide-screen TV took up the rest of it. Outside his windows, snow continued to fall in heavy sheets against the blackness of the night.

I put the plate of cookies on a glass coffee table then crossed to the aquarium where brightly colored fish swam around tall corral formations. "You weren't kidding about the fish."

He ran a hand through his hair. "My schedule is too crazy to have a dog, so I have fish."

It wasn't just any old fish tank. The aquarium must have been six feet long and rested on a shiny black cabinet with doors in the front. The glass was sparkling clean and the water crystal clear.

I glanced around as subtly as I could. His entire apartment was pretty spotless, aside from the pizza box on the counter separating the living room and kitchen. He might have been a single guy, but he wasn't a slob.

"So, it's just you and the fish for the holidays?" Kate asked, sinking onto one of the leather loveseats.

Alton grinned at her and nodded. "Right about now I'd rather have a dog."

"If you really want to borrow one, I'm sure we could arrange something," I said, thinking of Hermès running around like a miniature maniac in my apartment.

He laughed. "How's it going with being snowed in with all your friends?"

"It wouldn't be so bad if one of our neighbors hadn't been murdered," I said, watching his face for a reaction.

He immediately appeared chagrined. "You're right. It's awful what happened to Mr. Kopchek. They're sure it's murder?"

I decided to go out on a limb. "Pretty sure. It looks like he was poisoned."

"Really?" He looked genuinely surprised. "How?"

"Something he drank," I said.

Alton shook his head. "That's awful. I know the old guy wasn't the friendliest person in the building, but who would want to kill him?"

Kate shifted on the couch, crossing her legs. "Did you ever see him argue with anyone?"

Alton tilted his head at her, his gaze only dropping to her bare legs for a moment. "I'm not around during the day much, and I don't think the old man stays up late. I've never seen him when I've come home after closing the bar."

"And what about when you leave to open your place?" I asked. I'd run into him a couple of times in the middle of the day when he was headed out.

He shook his head. "I almost never ran into him, and if I did see him, he was always alone."

"Did you ever get citations?" Kate asked, stretching her arms wide along the couch cushions as she sat forward.

He looked confused for a moment, then he smiled. "You mean those tickets he gave out complaining about stuff? Yeah. He didn't like when I played music during the day. He thought it was too loud."

I instinctively looked down. Mr. Kopchek's living room would be right under us. I tried not to think of the body still lying on the couch. "Did you keep any of them?"

Alton cocked an eyebrow. "I think I tossed them in that bowl." He pointed to a bowl on the counter dividing the kitchen and the main living area.

"Do you mind if I look at them?" I asked, heading for the bowl that appeared to be mostly filled with change.

Another shrug. "Suit yourself. Just because he gave me tickets doesn't mean I wanted to kill him."

"I know," I said, fishing several crumpled pieces of paper from the bowl. "I got tickets, too, and I didn't kill him."

I unfolded the papers as Alton picked up one of the madeleines and took a bite.

"These are really good," he said. "A wedding planner and a baker."

Kate choked out a laugh. "Annabelle didn't bake those. If she bakes, it's only for stress relief, and it never tastes as good."

"Thanks," I said, shooting her a look then smiling at Alton. "Those were all Richard. We were lucky to get snowed in with a professional caterer."

"Were we?" Kate said under her breath.

He reached for another cookie. "My compliments to the chef then."

I took his distraction to shove the citations into my pocket. "We'd better head back. We just wanted to drop off the cookies." I motioned for Kate to follow me, and she popped off the couch.

When we reached the door, I opened it and stepped out into the hall. Alton held the door open, leaning against it with one arm stretched up against the doorframe. His hoodie rode up, and I saw a flash of a tattoo that stretched along one side of his torso.

"Thanks again for the cookies," he said.

I glanced away from his exposed skin quickly, feeling my face warming. "If you get bored hanging out with your fish, feel free to come upstairs."

"Will do," he said as he closed the door.

Kate followed me upstairs, only grabbing me by the sleeve when we reached my door. "Why did we leave so quickly? I thought the whole point was to question him about the time when he could have snuck into Mr. Kopchek's apartment."

I paused, listening for any sound in the stairwell. It was silent. "Because I found this." I pulled the citations out of my pocket.

"He told you about those." Kate looked at the formerly crumpled squares of white paper. "Mr. Kopchek didn't like him playing loud music."

I picked one citation out of the pile. "This one isn't for music. This one is for parking an SUV in the no-parking zone."

Kate stared at the paper then at me. "So? I guess he's also bad at parking."

I shook my head. "He doesn't drive an SUV."

CHAPTER FIFTEEN

Kate snapped her fingers. "How could I forget that he rides a motorcycle?" She frowned as she stared at the citation. "So why would he have one of Mr. Kopchek's complaints about parking an SUV? Do you think he took it off someone else's car?"

I gave her a withering look as I pushed open the door to my apartment. "Why would he do that?"

Kate was in mid-shrug when I turned and came face-to-face with my husband's broad chest. His arms were crossed, and his expression was stony.

"I tried to explain about the cookies," Richard called from the kitchen, "but he didn't buy it."

"I didn't buy it because I know you too well, babe," my husband said, his gaze never leaving me. "You and Kate went to our neighbor's to question him, didn't you?"

"Busted," Kate muttered to me under her breath.

"Before you get upset that I was investigating without you—" I started to say.

"Try that you were investigating at *all*," he corrected me. "We do have two detectives working on this case, and we both happen to be stuck in the building."

I looked over his shoulder to where his partner Hobbes sat at the dining table eating a second bowl of beef bourguignon. "But you're guys."

He tilted his head at me. "Thanks for noticing. What does that have to do with anything?"

"I wanted to talk to Alton with Kate. You know, use her super powers to figure out his deal."

Fern walked up and handed us each highball glasses filled with cranberry-colored liquid and topped with an elaborate garnish of leaves and berries hugging the rims that I hoped was edible—or at least not toxic. "It's true. I've seen her spot a cheating husband at a hundred paces."

Kate beamed at him, crossing her own arms. "It's a gift."

My husband let out a tortured breath, backing up to let us walk fully into the apartment. "So, did you?"

"Kind of," I said as I closed the door behind me. "We didn't get very far in questioning him, but we did get to check out his place."

"You should see his fish tank." Kate gave a low whistle as she flopped on the couch next to Buster and Mack, holding her drink high so it wouldn't spill. "And the place is spotless."

"How does that help the case?" Reese asked.

I took a sip of the cocktail Fern had handed me then held out my open palm. "Because we found this."

My husband took the citation and read it. "Okay. It's one of those tickets the old man gave out."

"It was in a pile of them that Alton said he'd gotten. He tosses them into a bowl on the counter. All the others were for playing music too loudly during the day."

"And this one is for parking an SUV half in a no-parking zone," Reese said then his eyes widened. "But the guy who owns the bar doesn't drive an SUV. He rides a motorcycle."

I took another sip of the sweet drink, wondering how much

booze was in it since I couldn't taste a thing. "See? Why would he have someone else's citation?"

"Because the person who got the citation was in his apartment and tossed it into the bowl," Kate said. "It totally explains the weird vibe I was getting off Mindy when she and her fiancé stopped by earlier. Now it makes total sense."

"What makes total sense?" Mack asked.

"Mindy and Alton are sleeping together," Kate said.

Buster and Mack both gaped at her, and Mack finally asked, "Who's Mindy?"

"Remember the bland guy who was here when you arrived?" Kate twisted to face them both. "Thinning hair, preppy."

Mack nodded. "He left with the other fellow who was…not preppy."

Kate grinned. "Exactly. Alton was the hot guy with the tattoos. Mr. Bland is engaged to Mindy, and Mr. Bad Boy is sleeping with her."

"You know this how?" Hobbes asked, walking up to join us.

"Simple," Kate told him. "They made a point not to look at each other when they were both here. If you really don't know someone, you don't avoid eye contact like that. They were hiding something. And if one of her tickets for badly parking her SUV was in Alton's apartment, and the ticket was written in the middle of the day when she's supposed to be at work, then it only makes sense that they're sneaking around behind her fiancé's back."

"Elementary, my dear," Fern said, his voice slightly slurred as he lifted his glass in salute and took a long swig.

"This is all getting to be a bit sordid." Richard came out of the kitchen with a plate of madeleines and put it on the coffee table. "Murder, affairs, spying. What kind of building do you live in, darling?"

"That's a good question," my husband said as he tapped one finger on his chin.

"Hey," I said. "This is a nice building. The murder and the affairs aren't a regular occurrence." I didn't mention the spying. With Leatrice as a longtime resident, that *was* a regular occurrence.

"We don't have evidence there is an affair," Hobbes said, clearly not convinced by Kate's expertise in body language. "And even if there is, it doesn't necessarily have anything to do with the murder."

"It does if Mr. Kopchek knew about it," I said. "You know how old people see everything that goes on. Just look at Leatrice."

"Speaking of the old girl," Richard pivoted, taking in the living room, "I thought it was unusually quiet in here."

"She and Sidney Allen decided to stay in their apartment after Hobbes and I questioned them." Reese pulled his phone out of his pants pocket. "It is pretty late. I think they were going to bed."

Kate put her hand over her mouth as she yawned. "I've lost all track of time."

"I don't know about anyone else," Richard smoothed his hands down the front of his Santa apron, "but I can't sleep knowing a murderer is galavanting around the building."

Fern put a hand to his throat. "You don't think the killer will strike again, do you?"

"I doubt we have a serial killer," Hobbes said. "From all appearances, Mr. Kopchek's murder seems targeted."

Buster shifted on the couch and his leather pants groaned. "We know that no one in here is the killer. If we stick together, we'll be safe."

"Will we?" Richard mumbled as he bustled back to the kitchen.

"Buster's right," my husband said. "Everyone should probably try to get some sleep. There isn't much more we can do tonight. I'm sure the rest of the building is sleeping already."

"I'll be heading home," Hobbes said. "There's a cruiser waiting for me outside."

"You sure?" my husband asked. "It's still snowing."

Hobbes cut his eyes to the crowded room and Fern refilling his cocktail as he hiccupped. "Positive."

Reese nodded and clapped him on the shoulder. "I'll let you know if anything develops."

Hobbes grabbed his coat from the stand. "And if I hear anything from the ME, I'll call you." He left with a cursory wave to the rest of us.

I glanced around the room. Hermès had nestled himself underneath the Christmas tree between a pair of red-and-green-striped boxes, and he was sleeping soundly. But unless anyone else fancied a spot under the tree, that meant I had to find places for Richard, Kate, Buster, Mack, and Fern to sleep. Although our one bedroom was considered roomy for George-town, it still wasn't huge. Just about the only place I could think to fit Buster and Mack was stretched out down the hallway. My mind went to the extra bed linens and blankets my mother had insisted on adding to our wedding registry. They'd be coming in handy tonight.

"The couch folds out," I said. "So, two people can sleep there."

Kate looked down at the cushion she was sitting on. "It does? How did I not know this? Who wants to share the foldout with me?"

Fern thrust his arm up, fluttering his hand wildly. "Me, me! Oh, this will be just like a slumber party."

My husband stepped closer to me and lowered his head to mine. "We don't have to share our bedroom, do we?"

I gave him a wicked grin. "You don't want Richard sleeping between us with Hermès at our feet?"

"Don't even joke about that," he said.

"Buster and I can sleep sitting up." Mack nodded to the over-sized armchairs across from the couch.

Buster bobbed his head up and down in agreement. "We can sleep anywhere. It's a talent we acquired on long bike rides."

"You can sleep while you ride?" Kate asked.

Mack held up a finger. "Only as a passenger."

"Less impressive," Fern muttered from behind his drink.

"I'll clear space on my office floor," I said, heading down the hall. "Reese has an air mattress we can put in there for Richard."

Richard's dark mutterings about the indignities of air mattresses faded as I reached the end of the hall and opened the linen closet. I pulled out all the sheets, blankets, and pillows we had, some of them still in their packaging. One nice thing about getting married and having a mother who believed in a fully-stocked registry—we did own just about every houseware we'd ever need.

My husband came up behind me and took an armload of pillows. "Not exactly how I imagined spending our first Christmas, although I can't say I'm totally shocked it ended up in a giant sleepover with your wedding friends."

"Don't look at me," I said. "Blame the blizzard. We were supposed to be in Charlottesville with my parents right now."

He smiled at me. "Don't even try to pretend you aren't happier here with all your friends."

I attempted a scandalized look. "You know I love my parents."

He leaned over, his lips buzzing against my earlobe. "I also know you love being in the middle of an investigation and being with your friends. Christmas with your parents would have been much quieter than this. For one, there wouldn't have been a murder."

I cocked my head at him. "Snowed in with my mother for days? We can't know that."

CHAPTER SIXTEEN

I sat up in bed and sniffed. Was I dreaming or did I smell coffee...and bacon?

I wasn't sure how long I'd been asleep, but it felt like my head had just hit the pillow. I twisted to look at the window where light was peeking from underneath the bottom corner of the pull-down shade. I groaned. How could it be morning already?

"What?" my husband mumbled next to me, lifting his head a millimeter off the pillow. "What's going on?"

"Nothing." I patted him on the shoulder. "I smelled something. I think Richard's already cooking."

"Cooking? I thought we saw him go to bed?"

He was right. We had watched Richard flounce off to sleep on the air mattress in my office, a drowsy Hermès tucked under his arm like a teddy bear. Since he'd been packed for a visit to my parents, he'd had pajamas to change into. Designer pajamas with a monogram. Unlike Kate and Fern, who'd both borrowed one of my oversized sleeping shirts. I was half afraid I'd find Fern with his hair in foam rollers tied up in a sleeping cap.

"I think he's starting breakfast. I smell bacon."

"Breakfast?" Reese let out a groan to match mine, opening one eye and then closing it again. "It's morning already?"

"Apparantly." I slid out of bed and stepped softly to the window, peeking under the shade and being momentarily blinded by white. The snow was no longer coming down in thick sheets, but there was at least two feet of it piled up everywhere. The cars in the back alley were white lumps, and there was no trace of a road.

I pulled a pair of black leggings on underneath my oversized UVA T-shirt and headed for the kitchen, pulling my bedroom door closed quietly as my husband had fallen asleep again. The man really could sleep through anything.

The aroma of coffee grew stronger as I walked down the hall, as did the sound of bacon sizzling.

"Finally," Richard said when I joined him in the kitchen. "I was wondering when someone else would wake up."

My best friend no longer wore his crisp blue pajamas. He'd dressed in equally wrinkle-free black pants and a forest-green button-down, all covered by the Santa apron from the day before. I didn't see Hermès, and I suspected the tiny dog was still sleeping.

I glanced at the kitchen wall clock. "It's only eight o'clock—and we went to bed after midnight."

"Maybe so, but I have an entire Christmas Eve dinner to prepare, not to mention prepping everything for Christmas Day and feeding people today." Richard opened the oven door and a blast of heat billowed out. "Oh good. My French toast soufflé is ready."

I stifled a yawn. "You're really going all in on this Christmas in the Chateau theme, aren't you?"

He cut his eyes to me as he donned oven mitts. "Don't be silly, Annabelle. French toast isn't French. It just happens to be a breakfast dish that holds well, and I have a feeling people will be waking up at all different times. I have no intention of being a short-order cook today."

I glanced through the opening between the kitchen and living room and saw no movement from the two lumps asleep on the foldout couch. Both Buster and Mack sat motionless in the overstuffed armchairs with their hands folded across their broad chests and their heads tipped back, eyes closed.

"And you aren't doing all this to wake everyone up?" I asked, giving him a pointed look.

He placed the soufflé casserole on a metal rack and tossed the oven mitts down beside it. "Hardly. Once everyone wakes up, my productivity will decrease dramatically. But I also couldn't sleep the day away with so much to do." He picked up a French press and poured coffee into a mug. "Christmas does not happen by itself, darling."

I opened the refrigerator door and plucked out one of my bottled Mocha Frappuccinos. "You know I appreciate everything you're doing, but I hate to see you working yourself to the bone. We don't have to have an elaborate Christmas, you know. We *are* snowed in. We can always keep things informal."

"Bite your tongue." Richard sucked in breath. "An informal Christmas? What's next? A wedding with hot dogs and tater tots? Really, Annabelle."

"Did someone say tater tots?" Kate lifted her head, her blond hair sticking up in several different directions.

Richard arched an eyebrow at me. "I rest my case."

I popped open the top to my Frappuccino and took a long swig of the cold drink, welcoming the sweet kick of caffeine. As much as I loved the smell of regular coffee, I preferred mine with plenty of mocha, milk, and sugar—and peppermint during the holidays.

"Since you're determined to put Martha Stewart to shame, is there anything I can do to help?"

He nodded to the living room where Kate was now sitting

up, and Buster and Mack were stretching their arms over their heads. "You can take them coffee." His gaze lingered on Kate's wild hair. "They're going to need it."

I poured coffee from the French press into two Christmas mugs and headed for the living room. "Caffeine, anyone?"

Buster and Mack both rumbled low as they sat up, and I handed the mugs to them.

"They aren't fancy cappuccinos like you make in your shop, but they should wake you up."

Mack put the red mug to his nose and inhaled deeply. "It's perfect."

"It's a holiday blend," Richard called from the kitchen. "It's got notes of spice cake and caramel."

"As long as it has caffeine," Buster murmured, sipping his coffee.

Fern raised his hand without sitting up. "I'll take mine Irish, please."

I shook my head. "The last thing you need is more booze."

"I beg to differ, sweetie. One shot of whiskey in my coffee, and I'll be good to go."

I eyed him lying in bed with an arm draped over his eyes. "You'll be under the table."

Kate ran a hand through her hair, smoothing down the wild locks. "You wouldn't happen to have any more of that hot chocolate, would you?"

Fern peeked one eye from under his arm. "That sounds good. I'll take my hot chocolate with a splash of Baileys."

I rolled my eyes. "No booze until afternoon. New house rule."

Fern let out a sigh. "It's afternoon in Europe. I thought this was a French-themed Christmas anyway."

I headed back to the kitchen where Richard was patting strips of bacon with a paper towel. "Your chateau theme is backfiring. Fern wants to observe European time and start drinking now."

"After last night, I don't blame him."

The murder came rushing back to me, and I shook the image of poor Mr. Kopchek out of my mind. "We've dealt with murder before. It's no reason to drink ourselves into oblivion."

"Is now the time to tell you that the French toast soufflé casserole is soaked in Grand Marnier?"

"Good," I said. "Fern can eat that instead of having a crack-of-dawn cocktail."

I scanned the counters, which were now filled with ingredients and serving dishes. "You didn't happen to see a Mason jar filled with hot chocolate mix, did you?"

Richard made a noise of surprise. "A Mason jar? I thought you had it out for Mason jars?"

"You know I have no problem with Mason jars used appropriately. It's when brides want to have Mason jars as vases for their luxury hotel weddings that it makes me crazy."

"And people say I'm persnickety," Richard said under his breath, then fluttered a hand toward the counter dividing the kitchen and living room. "I think I put it up there."

"And this Mason jar happens to be a gift." I spotted the jar and grabbed it, noticing that I only had about a third of the brown powdery contents left. "Mindy and Kurt gave them out to…"

Richard paused as he lifted a strip of bacon from the frying pan with a pair of tongs. "You really need more of your mocha, darling. You didn't even finish that sentence."

I stared down at the jar. "I just realized something. This could have been the murder weapon."

Richard dropped the bacon and it splattered on top of his shoes. He gaped at the jar in my hand then down at his feet. "My Prada loafers!"

CHAPTER SEVENTEEN

"Slow down, babe." My husband rubbed his eyes as I stood at the end of the bed holding the Mason jar. He was sitting up and leaning against the headboard with the sheets bunched around his waist. "I'm still waking up."

I tried not to get distracted by the fact that he was bare-chested, since he only slept in pajama bottoms. Forcing my gaze to stay on his face and not drift down to his impressive chest muscles, I did slow down. "Remember that I showed you the jar of hot chocolate mix that Mindy and Kurt gave all the neighbors?"

He nodded, his expression still sleepy. "I think so. It's the reason you had to call up Richard in a tizzy and order cookies."

"I wouldn't say tizzy."

My husband held up his palms as he swung his legs over the side of the bed. "I'm just repeating what Richard said."

"He said I was in a tizzy?" I frowned and cast a glance toward the door leading to the hall. "He's one to talk, especially after—"

"Babe?" My husband stopped me. "What about the hot chocolate mix?"

"Right." I waved the jar at him. "What if this was what was poisoned and not the cider Leatrice and Sidney Allen gave out?"

He scratched his hand over the dark stubble covering his cheeks. "It would be easier to introduce poison into a powder mix than into sealed bottles."

"Exactly. And those bottles have a screw top that's covered in foil. I know because Kate already drank ours."

My husband stood and stretched, and then I really had to work hard not to let my eyes drift. "So, your theory is that Mindy and Kurt poisoned the old guy using tainted hot cocoa?"

I cringed looking at the mix. "Pretty diabolical, right? But I don't think it was both of them. If Kate's right about Mindy messing around with Alton, then I'm sure she's the one who did the poisoning."

Reese padded over to the dresser and pulled a white T-shirt out of a drawer, tugging it over his head. "Even if Kate's right about the affair—and I'm not sure how we're going to prove that—you think Mindy killed Mr. Kopchek because he somehow knew?"

"Think about it," I said. "If Kate's also right that Kurt comes from money, maybe Mindy isn't in it for true love."

My husband dragged a hand through his hair and his one errant curl flopped back over his forehead. "They do seem like a bit of a mismatch, and I don't even have Kate's Jedi relationship skills."

"Say she got swept up by the bad-boy charm of the neighbor who owns a bar and started an illicit affair. The last thing she would want is for her rich fiancé to find out and call off the wedding."

Reese nodded. "It makes sense, but we don't have any evidence."

"Aside from the citation that was in Alton's apartment," I reminded him.

"Which might lend weight to the possibility of an affair but not a murder."

I sighed. "Mindy also had the opportunity to go into Mr. Kopchek's apartment and grab the mug. She left our apartment to go bake her pie. She could have snuck in, taken the mug and the Mason jar of mix, and gone back to her apartment without anyone noticing."

"I agree that your theory is solid, but we don't have proof."

I grinned. "You think I'm right?"

He looped an arm around my waist and tugged me so I was flush against him. "I've never said you weren't good at figuring out crimes. You did learn from an expert, after all."

I swatted at him playfully. "Are you saying you taught me everything I know?"

He leaned down and kissed me. "Something like that."

"You're impossible." I frowned at him even though his kiss made my knees wobbly. "I thought you hated me trying to solve cases."

He kissed me again. "I hate you constantly putting yourself in danger, babe."

I fought the urge to melt into him and instead peered up and drummed my fingers on his chest. "So how do we get proof?"

"The good news is we've all been snowed in since the murder. Nothing has gone out of this building aside from Mr. Kopchek's body." He opened our bedroom door. "The mug and the tainted hot chocolate have to be here somewhere."

"So, if Mindy's the killer, they're probably in her apartment." I followed him down the hall, thinking of ways I could casually search another resident's apartment without getting caught.

My husband stepped into the kitchen, and I followed him. Richard held up two oven-mitted hands to stop us.

"I'm in the middle of assembling my Bûche de Noël, and it's a very delicate process." He glanced over his shoulder at the chocolate sheet cakes on parchment paper. "Is there any way you can come back later?"

Reese cocked an eyebrow at him. "Give me some coffee, and I promise to stay out of your hair."

"Done." Richard pivoted to the French press and poured coffee into a mug then handed it to my husband.

I scanned the countertop. "Do you have any more of the soufflé? I didn't get to taste it yet."

Richard waved a hand toward the living room. "It's on the dining room table along with plates and silverware. Help yourself."

My husband took a sip of coffee as I pulled him out of the kitchen. "Soufflé?"

"Richard's been up for a while."

He took another long drink of coffee, already looking more awake. "While you try the soufflé, I'm going to hop in the shower."

I watched him head back down the hall for a moment before heading into the living room. Buster and Mack were at the table eating large squares of French toast soufflé, but there was no sign of Kate or Fern. Both the bathroom and office doors had been open, so I knew they weren't there.

"Please tell me Kate and Fern aren't making snow angels outside," I said to Buster and Mack as I stepped up to the soufflé and started to cut myself a piece.

"They're doing Richard's evil bidding," Mack said.

"I heard that," Richard called from the kitchen. "I just asked them to deliver some of my breakfast soufflé to the cute couple downstairs. I'm assuming her pie didn't cool in time for her to bring some up to us, but I'm holding out hope for that recipe. You know my best dishes are secret family recipes that I managed to sweet-talk out of people."

I dropped the knife into the casserole dish, and it clattered against the glass bottom. "Kate and Fern are downstairs with Mindy?"

"Not just her, unless her fiancé managed to tunnel his way through the snowdrifts," Buster said. "Why did you get even paler than usual, Annabelle?"

"Because if I'm right, they just took casserole to a killer."

Richard poked his head through the dividing space. "Did you say that Mindy is a killer?"

I nodded. "I don't have time to pull my husband out of the shower. Can you tell him where I went?"

I ran for the door as Richard threw down his oven mitts and followed me, yelling to Buster and Mack over his shoulder. "You heard her, boys."

CHAPTER EIGHTEEN

"I thought you hated this crime-solving thing," I said over my shoulder as Richard and I pounded down two flights of stairs.

"I do, but the faster it's over with, the faster I can get back to preparing Christmas Eve dinner. And I know you, Annabelle. You won't let it go until it's solved. If there's a problem, you have to fix it no matter what. It's both your best and worst quality."

"Thanks, I think."

"Not a compliment, darling, but you're welcome."

We reached Mindy and Kurt's apartment, and the door was standing open. I held out an arm to stop Richard and put a finger to my lips, miming that we should be quiet. I pushed the door open quietly and tiptoed inside.

The apartment was laid out similarly to mine, the front door opening into a single large dining and living space with a kitchen next to it divided by a pass-through counter. The room was slightly longer than mine and the kitchen seemed larger, but I noticed only two doors down the long hall toward the fire escape—presumably their bathroom and bedroom.

"Where are they?" Richard whispered as we stood inside the

main room, which looked like a spread from a Restoration Hardware catalog. It was so pristine and picture-perfect it was hard to believe people actually lived there. There was no Christmas tree, but glass hurricane candles ran the length of the dividing counter with greenery wound between them. "I smell the pumpkin pie."

The apartment did have the distinctive scent of cinnamon and nutmeg, and my head swung instinctively toward the kitchen where I spotted Mindy's head as well as Fern and Kate.

"It's my mother's recipe," Mindy said. "Do you want some whipped cream on top?"

Richard clutched my arm. "Is she serving them that pie she promised to bring us?"

"I'm a purist when it comes to hot chocolate," Fern said. "Unless you have some Baileys."

My stomach dropped. Hot chocolate? Was Mindy serving them hot chocolate? Had Kate or Fern let something slip? Did she know we were on to her? Was she attempting to get rid of anyone who might suspect her of poisoning Mr. Kopchek?

I ran to the kitchen, pulling Richard with me. When I spotted Kate putting a red mug to her lips, I swatted it away from her. It crashed to the linoleum floor, bouncing instead of breaking and sending brown liquid all over the floor and Kate's legs.

"Annabelle!" she screamed, hopping around as the hot droplets hit her. "What are you doing?"

"Saving your life," I said. "That hot chocolate might be poisoned."

Fern, who'd frozen as he was lifting his mug to his lips, slowly lowered it and put it on the counter, staring at it as if it was radioactive waste. He wore a plum brocade dressing gown with a matching ascot that made him look like a British Hugh Hefner. I was impressed he looked as stylish as he did since Kate still wore a sleep shirt over yesterday's miniskirt.

"Are these granite?" Richard whispered, touching a hand to the gleaming, dark counters and gaining a sharp look from me. "I know this is off topic, but this kitchen is considerably nicer than yours, darling."

Mindy gaped at me, ignoring Richard's comments. "Poisoned? Are you crazy?"

I shook my head. "We know you had a motive to kill Mr. Kopchek, and we also know that he was most likely killed by something he ate or drank. Since the mug he was using disappeared, that had to be the way he was killed. You gave him hot chocolate mix, which would have been an easy way to administer poison."

She put her hands on her hips. "Why would I want to kill an old man I barely knew?"

"Because he knew about you and Alton," I said.

Her cheeks reddened, and she visibly flinched. "I don't know what you're talking about."

I glanced at Kate for confirmation, and she gave me a single nod. "She definitely knows."

Mindy's murderous gaze shifted to Kate. "I'm not sure what you think you know, but I don't even know this Alton guy. Is he the guy who lives upstairs? The one who was in your apartment earlier?"

"Yeah," Kate said. "The one you went out of your way to ignore."

"And he's pretty impossible to ignore," Fern added.

Kate eyed her knowingly. "If I wasn't trying really hard to be monogamous, I'd be noticing him big time."

The flush on Mindy's cheeks deepened. "Like I said, I don't know him."

"Then why was one of your parking citations in his apartment?" I asked.

That made her mouth fall open a little bit, then she folded her arms over her chest. "No idea. Maybe he took it."

"Why would a guy who parks his motorcycle behind the building have any reason to take a parking citation off your car?" I asked. "And why would your SUV get a citation in the middle of the workday when you're supposed to be at work? Unless you have a reason to come back to the building for your lunch break."

"This is all guesswork." Mindy pressed her lips together. "You don't have any real proof."

"Proof of what?" Kurt stepped into the kitchen behind me, glancing at the spilled hot chocolate and at everyone's expressions. "Is everything okay in here?"

"They're accusing me of murder," Mindy said, her voice instantly taking on a frail, hysterical tone.

He crossed to her, putting an arm around her shoulders and glaring at us. "Murder? Of Mr. Kopchek? You came down here to accuse my fiancée of murder?"

"Actually, we came down to deliver some French toast breakfast soufflé," Fern said, waving at the plate of the golden-brown dish.

"I hope you like citrus," Richard added. "I might have gotten a tad enthusiastic with the Grand Marnier."

Kurt gave his fiancée a confused look, and she nodded her head at me. "The wedding planner is the one accusing me of murder."

"Mindy and I barely knew the man," he said. "Why would either of us kill him?"

I hesitated for a moment. Was I really sure enough to accuse her of sleeping with Alton in front of her fiancé? She was right that I didn't have hard proof, although there was circumstantial evidence and her obvious reaction when we'd mentioned him. Innocent people did not react like that.

"Because she wanted to make sure Mr. Kopchek couldn't tell you about the affair she was having with Alton," Kate said.

The room went silent for a beat, Kurt's expression freezing.

Then he turned to face Mindy. "The bar owner upstairs? Is this true?"

She shook her head vigorously, but her face was mottled red. "Of course not, hon. I was just telling them that I don't even know the guy."

From Kurt's expression, I could tell this news wasn't a total shock to him. Had he been suspecting something for a while and trying to convince himself he was imagining it?

"Our wedding is in a few months." His voice cracked. "I convinced my family that you didn't need to sign a prenup. You convinced me you didn't care about my money. Was all that a lie?"

Mindy's eyes were wild as she shook her head and grasped his hands. "Of course not. You have to believe me. All of *this* is a lie. I'm not involved with Alton. I had nothing to do with Mr. Kopchek's death, and I did not poison anyone's hot chocolate."

"I don't know about that."

Everyone spun as Reese came into the room. His dark hair was wet, with droplets of water dripping off his curls, and the white T-shirt half-tucked into his jeans was damp. "We now know the victim ingested your hot chocolate before he died."

CHAPTER NINETEEN

"How did he know the victim drank hot chocolate and not the cider?" Buster asked when we'd returned to my apartment.

"Apparently, the ME was snowed in and rushed the autopsy," Kate said, flopping down on the couch between the two leather-clad florists who were eating large servings of soufflé. "The tox report won't come back for a while, but they know Mr. Kopchek ate pizza and drank hot chocolate. Since his mouth and throat were swollen, they're positive he ingested the poison."

Mack shivered and eyed his plate. "What a horrible way to go."

"Death by cocoa," Kate said, making her voice sound dramatic and ominous.

"Don't worry," I said as Buster and Mack glanced at their mugs on the coffee table. "I'm not using the stuff Mindy gave me, although since Kate and I have been drinking it this week, I'm pretty positive it's safe."

"So where is your husband now?" Buster asked.

"Hobbes arrived right after Reese handcuffed Mindy," I said. "The streets are already being plowed, and he managed to get a cruiser through. They're searching her place now for the mug and Mason jar and the poison she could have used."

"This is all going so fast." Fern loosened the plum ascot around his throat. "I still can't believe a woman with such good hair could be a murderer. She doesn't even have frosted tips or bad roots."

"I don't think hair can indicate murderous intentions," I said.

Fern gave me a look that told me how wrong I was. "You'd be surprised, sweetie."

"Things are moving fast because a cop lives here," Richard called out from the kitchen as he poked his head through the opening. "I'm sure this case is getting preferential treatment. That makes me think. This building now has a great location *and* added security. I wonder when your old neighbor's apartment goes on the market."

Kate grinned at me. "If Mindy and Kurt break up and move out, maybe we can all move in."

I stifled a groan. As much as I adored my friends and colleagues, I did love having some breaks from them.

"I thought you hated the kitchens in this building," I reminded Richard.

"That's right. The kitchen in my place is too perfect to leave." He shrugged. "Oh, well. I suppose I'll just have to keep fighting for street parking when I visit you."

I let out a breath, more relieved than I wanted to admit. It was enough to have one nosy neighbor in Leatrice. I did not want to deal with more.

The door opened, and my husband came in followed by his partner Hobbes, who wore the same rumpled clothes he'd had on the day before.

"Any luck?" I asked.

"We found them," he said, his expression serious. "A corporate logo mug and a Mason jar of hot chocolate mix were out on their fire escape."

"Fire escape?" I naturally glanced toward the back of our apartment where the entrance to our fire escape was located. Although I'd used it before, it wasn't something I thought about often.

Hobbes nodded. "They'd been covered in snow during the night, but Mike thought we should sweep off the snow. There they were, buried under about two feet of powder."

"So, Mindy must have grabbed them from Mr. Kopchek's apartment and stashed them out there last night before her fiancé returned to their apartment," I said.

Reese nodded and frowned. "I doubt we'll get any prints off them since they were buried in snow, which started to melt once the sun hit it. They were pretty wet when I pulled them out."

"Sounds pretty open and shut to me," Kate said. "She had motive, opportunity, and you found the murder weapon on her fire escape."

"We're taking her down to the station to take a statement and book her," Hobbes said.

"Is she still claiming to be innocent?" Fern asked.

My husband ran a hand through his hair, which was still wet. "She copped to the affair, but she's keeping her mouth shut about the rest."

Kate sat forward. "She admitted to sleeping with Alton? I knew it!"

"Only because her fiancé accessed her cell phone and found text messages while we were searching." Hobbes wrinkled his nose. "It was not a pretty scene in the hallway."

"And I never got that recipe for her mother's pie," Richard said from the kitchen. "This day isn't turning out to be great for anyone."

I refrained from telling Richard that not getting a pie recipe wasn't quite the same as finding out your fiancé was both a cheater and murderer.

"What about Alton?" I asked. "Could he have been desperate to keep things going with Mindy?"

"No way." Kate shook her head. "Those two may have been doing the horizontal mambo, but I did *not* get the feeling that he was seriously emotionally attached to her."

"The horizontal mambo?" Richard said, making a face that told me exactly what he thought of that phrase.

"I'm keeping it clean." Kate glanced at Buster and Mack, who were known for their avoidance of curse words, as well as sin in general. "Would you rather I say fornicate?"

Richard shuddered. "Even worse."

"So far, it looks like Mindy was the one with the motive," my husband said. "And she did make the hot chocolate mix. Her former fiancé confirmed that she personally made and packaged all of them."

"Former fiancé?" Fern put a palm to his chest. "So much for getting to do her wedding hair in Newport."

"Poor Kurt," I said.

"Talk about a Christmas you'll never forget," Mack muttered.

"I'll question Alton since we need him to confirm the affair," my husband said, "but for now I'm going to go down and oversee the last of the search. So far we haven't found any poison that could have been used in the mix."

"No arsenic, strychnine, or cyanide?" I asked.

Reese cocked an eyebrow at me. "Should I be worried you have the names of poisons on the tip of your tongue?" Before I could answer, he went on. "Mr. Kopchek's reaction wasn't consistent with any of those poisons. And not all are powders. To mix into the hot chocolate without being noticeable, it would have been a powder."

"But since she made the mix earlier, she could have gotten rid of it," Hobbes said. "Even without finding the poison in her apartment, we have enough to book her."

My husband grabbed his coat off the hook. "I'll go into the station for a while, but I'll be back for dinner."

"You'd better." Richard waved a spoon at him from the kitchen. "You don't want to miss my Bûche de Noël."

Reese gave me a quizzical look.

"A cake that looks like a log," I whispered as I wrapped my arms around him.

"You're not selling it, babe," he whispered back, kissing me on the forehead. "But I'll be back as soon as I can."

After he and Hobbes left, Buster and Mack excused themselves to my office to FaceTime baby Merry and Fern stood, tugging the tassled tie of his brocade dressing gown. "Well, at least we solved the case before Christmas. This calls for a new signature cocktail."

I was going to say that it was still morning, but then I remembered that one of my neighbors was dead and another was being booked for his murder. "I'll drink to that."

CHAPTER TWENTY

"Did I sleep the day away?" Leatrice asked as I opened the door to my apartment holding a martini glass in one hand. "Is it already happy hour?"

"It's past noon on Christmas Eve," Kate said. "That means it's open season on cocktails."

"Try this, sweetie." Fern rushed up and handed her a glass filled with bright-green liquid. "I call it the Murderous Mistle-toe-tini."

I eyed Leatrice's red-and-white-striped jumpsuit and thought how much she looked like a candy cane. Her two-tone pink-and-white hair added to the bizarre effect. "Is Sidney Allen not joining us?"

Her wrinkled brow creased even more. "The last two days have been a lot for him. He's still recovering from the shock of being the last person to see Mr. Kopchek alive. I'm sure he'll join us later." She inhaled deeply. "It smells wonderful."

"Richard's been cooking all day." I dropped my voice. "Don't even think of going near the kitchen."

"But Christmas is tomorrow."

"But Réveillon is tonight," Richard called out from the

kitchen. "The French celebrate with their main meal late on Christmas Eve and it's called Réveillon."

I shrugged when Leatrice gave me a wide-eyed look. "You know Richard and his themed Christmases. He's going to pull off a Chateau Christmas if it kills him—or us. Just be glad it's not Christmas in the Casbah again."

Kate nodded from where she perched on the arm of the couch, lifting her martini glass high. "I could live a thousand lifetimes and never need to eat sweet potato couscous again."

"Too bad." Leatrice took a sip of her drink. "I have a belly-dancing costume I haven't worn in ages."

I said another small prayer of thanks that we weren't celebrating a casbah Christmas.

"I'm with Leatrice," Fern said, hooking an arm through hers. "This holiday theme isn't great for creative outfits."

"Isn't Christmas enough of a theme?" I asked.

Fern shrugged, then glanced down at Leatrice's hair. "You know what would lift my spirits? Finally doing something with your hair."

Leatrice put a hand to her two-tone hair. "I thought it was festive."

Fern wrinkled his nose. "One doesn't want one's hair to be too festive, sweetie." He led her over to the dining room table and plopped her down in a chair, whipping out a bag of hair supplies.

Leatrice looked a little taken aback, but she didn't protest as Fern unfurled a smock over her, and Hermès ran up and leapt into her lap.

Fern stood behind Leatrice assessing her hair and tapping one finger on his chin. "What did you think about your time as a platinum blonde? Did you really have more fun?"

Leatrice thought for a moment. "When I met my Honeybun, I had black hair, so maybe I have more fun as a brunette."

Fern nodded and rummaged through his bag of hair products again. "That might go with your coloring better, although we've never tried you as a strawberry blonde."

Leatrice's face brightened. "Like Nicole Kidman? Oh, I do like her."

"What's going on in here?" Richard walked out from the kitchen with his hands covered in oven mitts.

"Fern's going to make me into Nicole Kidman," Leatrice told him with a wink.

Richard stared at the heavily wrinkled woman. "This should be interesting." He dropped his voice to a mutter. "I hope he's got a time machine in that bag of tricks."

Fern popped his head up from searching in the bag and appraised Leatrice's hair again. "Maybe we should go with something more tried and true." He held up a tube of coloring. "Havana Brown should look fabulous."

"Sounds exotic," Leatrice said. "I'm sure I have an outfit that would work with that."

Fern's eyes widened. "Holidays in Havana. I love it!"

Richard stomped his foot. "No theme changing!"

Fern held up another tube. "I also have French Roast."

"Does her hair have to match the theme?" I asked.

Fern gave me a patient smile. "One does like to stay on point. The more I think about it, French Roast is perfect."

"Now I'm craving coffee," Kate said.

"As long as the smell of hair dye doesn't overpower the smell of my food." Richard spun on his heel and returned to the kitchen. "I'd hate to have to open a window in this weather."

Leatrice twisted around while Fern busied himself mixing up the hair color. "Where's your hubby, dear?"

"He and Hobbes took Mindy down to the station."

Leatrice set her drink on the table and patted the tiny Yorkie on the head. "Mindy from the second floor? Why?"

I'd forgotten that Leatrice had missed all our discoveries about Mindy and Alton and the police finding evidence on her fire escape. "It's kind of a long story, but she's the one who killed Mr. Kopchek."

Leatrice gaped as Fern began applying hair color and folding each strand of hair in tinfoil. "I can't believe it. She seemed like such a nice girl. Why would she want to kill him? Was this about the tickets he gave her fiancé about the bike? Sidney Allen and I told Kurt it was fine by us if he left it on the first floor, and it's not bothering anyone but—"

"It's not about the bike." I cut her off. "She and Alton were having an affair, and Mindy killed Mr. Kopchek because he knew about it."

"They were?" She turned her head and Fern turned it right back. "How did I miss that?"

Kate shrugged. "You're looking for spies. They weren't spying."

"Still." Leatrice shook her head, which made Fern frown. "I should have been more attentive to what was going on in our building. I wonder how Mr. Kopchek knew and I didn't."

"He did live beneath Alton." Kate took a long swig of her drink. "My guess is that he heard more than he wanted to."

Leatrice's cheeks flushed under her heavy coral rouge. "Goodness. That must have been distressing."

Fern took a break from applying hair color and wiped his forehead with the back of his hand. "Wouldn't have bothered me."

"Or me," Kate said. "That's why I have noise canceling headphones."

The scent of hair dye wafted across the room, and my eyes watered. "He gave Mindy parking citations during the day, so maybe he put two and two together. Or maybe he spotted her going into Alton's apartment. However, he figured it out, he knew. And Mindy knew he knew."

"But why kill him?" Leatrice asked.

"Because Mindy's fiancé is rich, and she'd convinced him they didn't need a prenup," Fern said, waving his hair dye brush.

"And Kurt was way more into her than she was into him," Kate added.

"If Mr. Kopchek talked, it would ruin her chance to have a wealthy husband," I said.

Leatrice tapped a bony finger on her chin. "I wonder if she was going to use her rich husband's money to save her lover's bar?"

I nearly spluttered as I took a drink. "What do you mean?"

"That handsome fellow's bar is in serious debt," Leatrice said matter-of-factly. "He's about to go under."

Kate's eyebrows popped up. "How do you know this?"

"Please don't say your dark web hacker friends," I muttered under my breath like an incantation.

She grinned at me, her tinfoil hair making her look slightly space-age. "You're such a good guesser, Annabelle. Boots and Dapper Dan did a little digging for me after I got online last night and told them what happened."

"Was any of this digging illegal?" I immediately held up a hand. "Wait. Don't tell me. I don't want to know."

"I really didn't ask, dear." Leatrice took another sip of her drink and grimaced. "I do know that they accessed bank records and discovered just how deeply in debt he is. And he has at least one loan he personally guaranteed."

"Which means the creditors can come for his personal possessions," I muttered, more to myself than to anyone else.

Kate locked eyes with me. "Do you think this could have something to do with the murder?"

"It would explain why Mindy felt she needed to kill the old man. If she was serious about Alton and he told her about his money troubles, she might have been planning to help him out once she'd gotten married."

"So tawdry." Fern shook his head as if he disapproved, but his eyes glittered, and I knew he was loving the scandal.

"We've been assuming it was all Mindy since she had the most to lose," I said. "But this means Alton could have easily been in on the whole thing with her."

Fern's gleeful expression morphed to concern. "Just how many people in this building are killers?"

"I need to tell Reese." I pulled my phone from my jeans pocket and speed dialed him, grumbling when it went to voicemail. "He must be dealing with Mindy."

I left him a message about Alton and hung up. "Do you think we should try to question him or at least keep him busy until Reese can get back here to talk to him?"

"You can't," Leatrice said, the tinfoil swinging around her head as she shook it. "I saw him leave the building when I was on my way up."

"Leave the building?" Kate glanced at my windows which still showed a world covered in white.

"The snowplow had already been by once," Leatrice told her. "You can't hear since you're all the way on the fourth floor."

"He must have gone to his bar," I said. "He did tell me the holidays are a busy time for him."

"Or he's making a run for it," Fern said.

We all turned our heads to him, and he bobbed his shoulders up and down. "What? If my accomplice was being questioned by the police, I know I'd be making a run for it."

"Same," Kate said.

I pulled my phone out. "Should I tell Reese that he's trying to get away?"

"We don't know that for sure, dear," Leatrice said.

"You're right." I hesitated as I stared down at my phone's screen. I didn't want to call in a false alarm. The man could be innocent and just checking in on his bar.

"One way to find out," Leatrice said. "We take a peek into his apartment and see if it looks like he left it for good."

I narrowed my eyes at her. "Please tell me you didn't make a copy of everyone's key in the entire building."

She fluttered a hand at me. "Don't be silly. I mean we can peek into his place through the fire escape."

"I don't know—" I started to say but Fern had already spun on his heel and was heading toward the back of my apartment and my fire escape.

"Even if we can't see a thing, we'll have gotten out of the apartment for a while," he said over his shoulder. "And I don't know about the rest of you, but I'm going stir crazy."

"We peek in the window and come right back up," I said, following him reluctantly.

"Of course." He tossed back the rest of his drink and winked at me over his shoulder. "What else would we do, sweetie?"

CHAPTER TWENTY-ONE

"This was a bad idea." I stamped my feet and rubbed my arms briskly.

We'd managed to slip and slide our way down the fire escape to the floor below and Leatrice, Fern, Kate, and I stood huddled outside Alton's back door.

"It was a bad idea not to wear boots," Kate said as she stood in a pile of snow that reached mid-calf.

There was a window to one side, and Leatrice had her face pressed to the glass with her hands on either side. "I can't see a thing, but all the lights are out."

The tinfoil covering her head did not make us a less conspicuous or odd-looking bunch. And the ammonia scent had me standing as far away from her on the fire escape as I could get.

"What about the aquarium?" Kate asked. "He had fancy lights in that."

I glanced at my assistant. "You noticed aquarium lighting?"

She shrugged one shoulder. "I used to date a guy who was into aquariums. I recognized the ambient lighting setup."

"No aquarium lighting that I can see," Leatrice said, straightening. "But this window is pretty fogged up."

"Well, we tried." I turned to the metal stairs. "Time to go back in."

"If only we could peek inside," Leatrice said then let out a small yelp. "Look, his window is unlocked."

I pivoted back around. Leatrice held the windowpane open, and her aluminum head was disappearing inside the apartment.

"What are you doing?" I hissed.

"Looking for clues," she said, her voice muffled from her head being inside.

"Maybe the poison is in here," Kate said. "Reese didn't find anything in Mindy's apartment."

"You know what my husband would say about this." I nibbled my bottom lip as Leatrice disappeared entirely into Alton's apartment.

"You're under arrest?" Fern said, giggling and then hiccupping and slapping a hand over his mouth.

"Pretty much." I'd done plenty of things that were quasi-legal in my pursuit of criminals, but I knew it drove my cop husband crazy, and I'd promised to stop.

"Then you stay outside, and we'll look for clues," Kate said stepping through the window. "I, for one, don't like the idea of a guy like Alton getting away with murder."

Man, she really did not like Alton.

Fern and I stood on the fire escape for another minute, shivering and looking at each other until he finally patted me on the arm. "Sorry, sweetie. I'm going in just to warm up."

I huffed out a breath and it formed a cloud of steam in front of me. "Fine. If you're all going in…" I followed him through the window, allowing my eyes a moment to adjust to the darkness.

We were inside the main room of the apartment. I could make out outlines of his dark furniture and of my friends moving around. Kate was easy to track because she was using her cell phone as a flashlight.

"Anything?" I asked.

"What exactly are we looking for again?" Fern asked.

"Some sort of powdered poison that could have been blended into the hot chocolate mix," I whispered.

"I'll check under the kitchen sink," Leatrice said, her shadowy figure groping along the walls.

Kate fumbled with something in the living room, and then her flashlight illuminated the fish tank. More specifically, the cabinet under the fish tank.

"Bingo," she said.

"What is all that?" I squinted at the plastic containers and jugs.

"Supplies for an expensive fish tank." Kate rummaged around until she found something and lifted it up. "Including some stuff to clean the tank that comes in a powder form. It's purply, but I'm sure it could be blended into dark brown cocoa."

"And is that stuff poison?" I asked, my heart racing.

"If it cleans fish tanks, I'm pretty sure it isn't good to ingest." Kate held her phone's light up to the label on the white plastic jug. "Potassium permanganate. And it's got a nice toxic warning on it."

"We should take that to Reese," Leatrice said from the kitchen. "There's nothing in here."

"Let's go." I waved at Kate even though she couldn't see me in the dark. "I do not want to be here if Alton comes back—"

My word trailed off as the front door open, and the lights came on. I glanced back at the window. Fern was already outside, but there was no way Kate and Leatrice could make it in time.

Alton walked into the apartment, stopping in mid-stride when he saw me. Then he swiveled his head to Kate and the plastic jug in her hand and his jaw tightened.

"What are you two doing here?"

At least he hadn't seen Fern leaving through the window and

didn't know Leatrice was in the kitchen, although her head smelled so pungent he'd soon be able to smell her.

I decided to go with honesty. "We know that you helped Mindy poison Mr. Kopchek."

Kate opened and closed her mouth, but Alton didn't react.

"Why would I have anything to do with that man's death? I barely knew him."

"But he knew about you and Mindy, didn't he?" I pressed, making a point not to look at Leatrice's head popping over the kitchen divider.

His expression remained unconcerned. "The brunette who popped into your apartment with her fiancé? I know her about as well as I did Mr. Kopchek."

"That's not what she's telling the cops right now."

That did it. His confident smile faltered.

"They're questioning her about killing Mr. Kopchek to keep him quiet about your affair," I continued. "Her fiancé knows everything, by the way. Your girlfriend won't be marrying a rich guy and bailing out your bar, after all."

"So, it was all for nothing?" Alton glowered at me for a moment before turning and running back down the short hallway to his front door.

I was so startled, it took me a second to realize that he was trying to get away. "Stop!"

As he ran past the kitchen doorway, Leatrice launched herself at him, but he shrugged her off his back, and she landed with a hard thud on the floor. Kate and I both rushed to her as Alton dashed out the door.

"Are you okay?" I asked Leatrice, putting a hand under her elbow to lift her.

She waved me off. "I'm fine. You can't let him get away."

Kate and I ran out of the apartment, hearing footsteps on the stairs going down.

"Stop!" I yelled again and peered over the railing. He had a full flight of stairs head start on us.

Nevertheless, I hurried down, gripping the handrail to keep from slipping. Kate was right beside me, holding the other handrail. When we reached the ground floor, I almost slipped off the last step.

Alton hadn't made it outside. Daniel Reese was scuffling with him near the door. I didn't know why he was there, but he must have heard me screaming.

"He's a murderer," I yelled, as Daniel struggled to keep him from leaving.

Kate's eyes were huge as the two men fought. I looked around for something I could use to help Daniel, but there was nothing in the bare foyer. Then Alton reached around for something jammed in the waistband of his pants, and I only realized it was a gun when I heard the sharp crack.

Kate screamed, and we both ducked. The men dropped to their knees, and the gun clattered to the floor and was kicked to the side.

My skin went cold, and I squeezed my eyes shut. If my brother-in-law had been shot trying to catch a killer we'd been chasing, I'd never forgive myself. When I opened my eyes, Daniel was standing, and he had Alton in a headlock, the bar owner's face purple.

I scanned the floor for the gun and scooped it up, pointing it at Alton even though my hands were shaking. Footsteps pounded behind us, and within moments everyone from my apartment was jammed into the foyer.

Alton finally went limp, and Daniel let him sink to the floor. Buster and Mack pushed through the group and each took one of his arms, their expressions deadly. For his sake, I hoped Alton stayed unconscious until the police came for him.

I finally lowered the gun and Leatrice took it from me,

patting me on the arm. "Why don't I take this, dear? You look like you might drop it."

Kate launched herself into Daniel's arms, and he staggered back in surprise, wrapping his arms around her.

When she pulled back, her face was streaked with tears. "I thought I'd lost you."

"I'm fine," he said, his voice husky. "You didn't lose me."

Kate kissed him, her hands raking through his dark hair flecked with silver at his temples.

"Well, well, well," Fern said from behind me. "This explains a lot."

"Another Reese brother," Richard said with a sigh. "And another person for dinner."

"At least he's a silver fox," Fern said, his eyebrows arching. "Merry Christmas to me."

CHAPTER TWENTY-TWO

"You didn't know your brother was coming?" I asked my husband as I cuddled with him on the couch later that evening.

He shook his head, glancing at his older brother standing next to the Christmas tree with Kate. The two had been inseparable since he'd taken down Alton, and I wasn't sure Kate was ever going to unwrap her arms from his waist. Even though I wasn't used to seeing Kate attached to one man for so long—or for longer than an hour—I liked the look of the two of them together. And since everyone had stopped openly gaping, Daniel looked pretty content.

"I told him what happened, but he never let on he was planning to come across town to our place." Reese lowered his mouth to my ear. "Did you know they were dating?"

"Not until recently." I didn't need to drop my voice because Big Bad Voodoo Daddy's retro swing version of "Jingle Bells" was playing pretty loudly, and Hermès yipped along to the music as he scampered around the tree. I was amazed the little Yorkie could still move so quickly considering how much of Richard's Christmas Eve dinner everyone had slipped him under the table.

My husband pulled me closer. "Well, I'm glad he was here. What I'm not happy about is you and your friends deciding it was safe to climb into a killer's window."

"We didn't know for sure he was a killer when we went in. And we never planned to go in—at least I didn't. But the window was unlocked and Leatrice went inside…"

I cast a quick glance at my neighbor who sat wedged next to Sidney Allen in one of the armchairs. Fern had rinsed and dried her now mocha-brown hair in time for dinner, and I had to admit it was a flattering color. It had been a surprise for Sidney Allen, but he seemed to take it in stride after all the shocks over the past two days, although he did look more subdued than usual. Luckily, Leatrice had talked enough for both of them, regaling everyone with a blow-by-blow account of us confronting Alton and Daniel taking him down in the foyer.

My husband tilted his head down to look at me. "Are you going to claim peer pressure as your defense? Remember, babe, I know you pretty well."

My cheeks warmed. "No, but in my defense, I did call you first. And I argued against going inside the apartment. Kate and Fern can back me up on that."

"Forgive me if I don't consider them the most reliable sources," he muttered as Fern sailed through the living room carrying a tray of martini glasses filled with both of his signature drinks—the Blizzitini and the Murderous Mistletoe-tini. He'd changed from his brocade dressing gown and wore a powder-blue velvet suit that reminded me of Jack Frost. Even the enormous blue topaz ring on his finger glittered like ice.

"I thought you'd be glad we caught the real killer," I said. "You almost booked an innocent person for murder."

"I wouldn't say innocent," Richard said as he perched on the arm of the couch next to us. He'd finally taken off his Santa apron and looked more relaxed now that dinner was over, and he'd been given a heavy helping of compliments on the impressive spread of food. "Mindy did have an affair with one of her neighbors."

"But she actually didn't have anything to do with Mr. Kopchek's murder," I reminded him. "I'm not saying she wasn't a gold digger, but she wasn't the one who put the potassium whatever in Mr. Kopchek's hot chocolate mix. We're just lucky Kate dated a guy with a fancy fish tank and knew something about the chemicals you use."

Richard mumbled something about the odds being in our favor considering Kate's dating history, but I ignored it.

"I should have questioned the evidence being on the fire escape more," my husband said, shaking his head. "It wasn't hard for Alton to climb down and put it there and then for the snow to cover his tracks."

I patted his hand. "Don't beat yourself up too much. Mindy seemed like the more obvious villain."

"Speak for yourself," Richard said. "I never trusted Alton. Like I said, too many tattoos."

"Did he really think that Mindy was going to save his bar after she was married?" I asked. "And it was worth killing over?"

My husband shrugged. "That's what he said when he finally spilled his guts at the station. The guy wasn't a criminal mastermind as much as he was desperate."

I rubbed my arms as I thought about poor Mr. Kopchek. "That makes it even scarier."

"People kill over much less," Reese said. "If the bar was his whole life, and he'd sunk every penny into it, I'm not surprised he was desperate to save the thing. He must have seen Mindy as a lifeline."

"And she was swayed by his bad-boy charm." Richard made a tsk-ing noise in the back of his throat. "What did I tell you, Annabelle? Bad boys are never a good idea."

"You don't have to tell me," I said. "I married a cop."

"Upon my excellent advice," my best friend said, clearly

remembering things a little differently than I did and forgetting how long it had taken him to warm up to Reese.

"I'm just grateful you were around, Richard," my husband deadpanned, which earned him a sharp jab in the ribs.

"You don't have to thank me." Richard waved a hand. "If you weren't here, I might be sharing the holidays with a tattooed band leader."

I glared at Richard and tried to steer the conversation away from my past. "It's too bad Mr. Kopchek threatened to tell Kurt." I remembered what my husband told me that Mindy had finally confessed at the station. "If he hadn't, he might still be alive."

Richard frowned. "Mindy might not have killed the old man, but she withheld evidence from the police when she suspected what happened."

"She did say she was terrified that she'd be implicated," my husband said.

Richard snorted out a laugh. "More like she was scared to reveal the affair and get dumped by her rich fiancé."

I was with Richard on this one. Mindy might not have poisoned the old man, but she'd started the ball rolling by messing around and hiding it. And when he'd died and she suspected her lover might have been involved, she did nothing.

"Don't worry. She's being charged with obstructing an investigation," Reese said.

"Good." Richard smoothed his hands down the front of his shirt. "As much as I wanted her pie recipe, I'd hate for justice not to be served."

"Speaking of serving." Fern swept his tray down at our eye level. "You two look like you could use a drink."

Reese and I both took a glass from the tray, careful not to spill the bright-green and cherry-red contents. Richard glanced up at the clock on the wall and put his hands to his cheeks. "That reminds me. It's almost time for me to set out the dessert buffet."

"Dessert buffet?" I put a hand to my stomach. "Didn't we just finish dinner?"

Richard shot me a dismissive look. "Over an hour ago. Besides, we can't have a proper Christmas at the Chateau without a dessert display."

"I am looking forward to the log cake," my husband said.

"Sacre bleu!" Richard sucked in a sharp breath. "I hope you aren't referring to my Bûche de Noël as a 'log cake.'"

"It *is* a cake that looks like a log," I argued as Richard tapped one toe rapidly on the floor.

"I'm going to pretend I didn't hear that." Richard spun on his heel and flounced off to the kitchen.

"Good news." Mack appeared from the back of my apartment where he and Buster had been FaceTiming with the young woman they'd taken underwing. "The snow has been cleared enough that Prue and Merry will be able to join us for Christmas morning."

"Which is a good thing," Buster added, coming up behind Mack. "Because Santa delivered all their presents here." He gestured to the tree with a wink, and I noticed there were more wrapped boxes than there had been.

Leatrice clapped her hands. "It will be so much fun to watch Merry open her presents. Last year she was a baby, but this year she'll actually be able to rip the paper."

"She growing up fast," Buster said, his voice more gravelly than usual.

"Too fast." Mack dabbed at his eyes. "Christmas really is more fun when you get to see it through a child's eyes."

"No crying," Fern said, pushing cocktails into Buster's and Mack's hands. "It's Christmas Eve! Even though the weather is dreadful, and everyone's plans were messed up, we're all together."

"And we solved a murder," Leatrice added.

"That's right." Fern lifted his cocktail. "Which makes it kind of a perfect Wedding Belles holiday party, if you ask me."

I stifled a groan. "Let's not make it a habit, though."

"Please," my husband murmured from behind his drink.

"A toast to the best blizzard Christmas ever!" Fern lifted his martini glass even higher.

"It's Christmas at the Chateau," Richard cried as he came out of the kitchen holding a tray of iced cookies, gingerbread madeleines, and sugary palmiers.

We all raised our glasses and drank as Richard muttered about his theme being hijacked.

"I have another toast."

We all turned to see Daniel holding his glass up. He cleared his throat. "I'd like to raise a glass to the talented, beautiful woman who figured out the pivotal clue and helped put away a killer."

Kate's cheeks flushed as she locked eyes with him.

"To Kate." He took both of her hands in his and dropped down onto one knee. "The woman I hope will agree to be my wife."

"Son of a nutcracker!" Mack said in a hushed rumble, as Kate's mouth dropped open.

The room was silent for a moment, then Kate bobbed her head up and down and threw her arms around Daniel. "Yes! Of course, yes!"

Reese quietly choked on his drink as Fern's own martini glass tipped over and the contents splattered onto my hardwood floor. Daniel had barely gotten to his feet when Fern danced over to them both, pulling them into a hug and sloshing the rest of his cocktail all over the wrapped gifts.

I managed to shake off my shock and jump up, making my way over to Kate and holding my arms out. "I can't believe it!"

"I know," she said as she untangled herself from Fern's hug, her eyes bright with tears. "We're going to be sisters."

I shook my head through my own tears. "We already are."

Then we hugged as tears streamed down both of our faces. My husband pulled his brother into a bear hug, Richard wrapped his arms around both of them, and Fern and Leatrice grabbed me and Kate from behind. Buster and Mack came up behind them, and then everyone was hugging and jumping up and down together with Hermès yipping maniacally and Richard shrieking that his designer loafers were getting trampled.

"This really is the best worst Christmas ever!" Leatrice cried from somewhere in the crush of bodies.

It was good to know that as much as things changed, some things—like the spirit of Christmas and my crazy friends and how much we meant to each other—never would.

———

Thank you for reading *Slay Bells Ring!*

This book has been edited and proofed, but typos are like little gremlins that like to sneak in when we're not looking. If you spot a typo, please report it to: laura@lauradurham.com
Thank you!!

ABOUT THE AUTHOR

Laura Durham has been writing for as long as she can remember and has been plotting murders since she began planning weddings over twenty years ago in Washington, DC. Her first novel, BETTER OFF WED, won the Agatha Award for Best First Novel.

When she isn't writing or wrangling brides, Laura loves traveling with her family, standup paddling, perfecting the perfect brownie recipe, and reading obsessively.

Find her on:
www.lauradurham.com
laura@lauradurham.com

To get notices whenever she releases a new book, follow her on BookBub:

ALSO BY LAURA DURHAM

Annabelle Archer Series:

Better Off Wed

For Better Or Hearse

Dead Ringer

Review To A Kill

Death On The Aisle

Night of the Living Wed

Eat, Prey, Love

Groomed For Murder

Wed or Alive

To Love and To Perish

Marry & Bright

The Truffle with Weddings

Irish Aisles are Smiling

Godfather of Bride

Claus for Celebration

Bride or Die

*Annabelle Archer Collection: Books 1-4

Annabelle Archer Books available as Audiobooks:

Better Off Wed

For Better Or Hearse

Dead Ringer

Review to a Kill

Annabelle Archer Collection: Books 1-4

———

To get notices whenever I release a new book, follow me on BookBub:

https://www.bookbub.com/profile/laura-durham

Made in the USA
Middletown, DE
27 November 2020

25445925R00085